To Take a Throne

TO TAKE A THRONE

JESSICA GREYSON

BLAINE, MINNESOTA

ONE

I can't believe you're abandoning me for a pretty maid," chided Eliot, following Ransom to collect his things from the tent.

Ransom laughed lightheartedly, lifting the flap and entering the tent. "Just wait for your turn, Eliot."

"What? You think a maid will turn my head?" scoffed Eliot, flopping down on his cot. "You've got the only interesting maid I've seen in two or three kingdoms."

"And she's mine," said Ransom, turning from his pack with a smile.

"I do think I would have gotten the job done a little faster than you have."

"Well, I for one I am grateful you didn't have this job, and I think Annabeth would agree with me."

"Really, this whole thing would have been over a lot sooner but I was too busy and then I had to come in and clean up your mess . . . as *always.*"

"My mess? Always! I am not the one who dragged her to that horrible villain and . . ."

Eliot raised his hand. "I see we shall never agree on the whole matter. Perhaps you're right," sighed Eliot, settling back on his cot. "Besides, if we keep talking this over, you'll never be ready, and I'd hate to be the reason that Annabeth is kept waiting."

Ransom grinned, swinging his pack on his shoulder. "We've had a good run, you've always had my back and we had plenty of adventures together, but now our paths turn, so until we meet again, ol' friend, Godspeed to you and may you find a wife who makes you feel like a king."

"Is that what Annabeth makes you feel like?"

There was no wiping the smile from Ransom's face. "Better."

"Ransom?" It was Annabeth's voice outside of the tent flap.

"I am coming, my love."

Eliot rolled his eyes. As Ransom left the tent, his arm slipped around Annabeth's waist, drawing her close and dropping a kiss on her lips, causing a rosy blush to rise in her cheeks that were still pale from time to time. Life had been cruel to her but she had survived and was starting a new chapter with Ransom at her side, to be her protector and love.

With an arm wrapped around one another they stepped out of his sight. Eliot flopped himself back down on his cot. When one was on a mission sleep wasn't always the easiest to come by, and there was no knowing when his king would need him again, so he would sleep, eat, and practice with his sword until he was needed again, and right now seemed the perfect time for a nap.

"Eliot sir?" It was the sound of a page at the tent flap—a young page at the sound of it. Eliot sir indeed.

"Yes," he yawned with a stretch.

"The king has sent for you."

Rolling to his feet, Eliot looked down at the page with a lifted eyebrow as the boy looked up at him in wonder. He waited a moment for the boy to lead the way. The page did not move.

"Yes?"

"Oh?" said the page, still not moving.

Eliot held back the corner of his mouth from smiling at the boy's wide-eyed awe.

"Lead on then," he commanded.

"Yes!" said the boy, leaping into motion and charging in the direction of the king's tent. He very well could have gone there himself, but a page in training was something to be handled carefully; the boy needed to learn how to take responsibility, and next time it might not be him—but perhaps an overbearing lord or a foreign ambassador he was sent to fetch.

Reaching King Fredric's tent, the small page stopped at the tent flap. "Just a moment if you please, I'll make sure the king isn't occupied."

Eliot nodded, tucking his hands behind his back.

A moment later the boy appeared. "He will see you now."

Eliot entered and bowed low to his king.

"Eliot, I am sorry to be sending you out again so soon. I've received word that Chambria is in need of our help, and you're the only one at hand as well as the closest to Raven Castle."

"I am willing, my king, but I am curious as we have no treaty with Chambria."

"Not at this moment, but we soon will. It seems that Lord Raburn was in league with the Lord Chancellor of Chambria and set up a coup. The king and queen were slain, along with their second son, but the heir and his sisters escaped to Raven Castle. I cannot send my current men to war very easily after bringing them so close to home. However, I am sending you to fetch Princess Regina; my son is in need of a wife and eventually an heir."

"A marriage of alliance, in exchange for our fighting men?"

"I wouldn't interfere, but I knew the king of Chambria, and he was nothing but a kind man. The Lord Chancellor is quite a different story. If even half the tales I've heard are true. I do not wish for such a neighbor. Power hungry monsters never do anyone good."

"At once, Your Majesty?"

"I've sent for them to have your horse saddled and a food pack ready. I'll see you at home in less than a week, I suspect. We will give the soldiers who have been guarding the home front a day to toast my son and his new bride and have them sent across through the mountain. Once it's put down, they can come home to their families. I hate to keep my men fighting more than I must."

"Then I leave at once, Your Majesty."

"Thank you."

King Fredric dismissed him with a wave of his hand.

"Oh! The king of Belterra knows what is going on. You of course have full freedom to circle into Belterra on your way to and from Raven Castle—not that we needed it but considering the situation."

"Thank you, Your Majesty."

The king nodded and Eliot stepped out of the tent. The page was standing there holding on to his black horse's bridle.

"He's ready, sir, provisions and all."

"Thank you," said Eliot, leaping into the saddle and taking the reins. He nodded to the young page and kicked the horse into a loping canter.

Crossing the stream where they had defeated Lord Raburn and his men a few days before, he speed across the open fields and through the thickening forest, reaching the mountain pass that led up to Raven Castle.

TWO

Princess Regina looked down the mountain cliff, to the city below as darkness crept into the valley as the sun set. The last thing it would touch in Chambria before it set was Raven Castle. The light of torches lined the city walls and nested within was the castle outlined by the flames on the palace walls. Chambria, her home, her people, her place.

Why must I be so far removed from this situation, why is Arthur keeping me at a distance? Why do people rebel? Why does power corrupt?

She turned from her window and paced back and forth trying to think, to process, to sort through the emotions storming through her heart. Everything had happened so quickly; she still couldn't piece it all together.

Her father's cup falling from his hand at dinner.

Her mother's panicked scream being cut short.

The dart that flew through the air with a cunning whistle.

Half of the men at the tables rising with a war cry.

The few loyal gathering around them, pushing them to safety, the soldiers skirmishing—unsure who was friend and who was foe.

Essie clinging to her tightly, Richard pushing them forward, Arthur blazing a path with his blade. The jostling, shoving . . . the break in the men. The blade coming toward her, and the one who held it . . . She closed her eyes, shielding Essie with her body.

Then . . . Richard's cry.

A shiver ran through her body.

It kept playing over and over in her mind, day, night, morning, nightmare. She could hear it anywhere and everywhere. He had rushed forward and shielded her with his body, blocking the deathly blow with his own life. Arthur had pulled her ahead and she had glanced over her shoulder . . . his blue eyes. Her heart twisted, the pain, agony, anger, and love, they were all there. The last words from his lips. "Go!"

She turned and pounded her fists into the stone wall.

"No! No! No!" She kicked the wall and her foot throbbed, and she sank to the floor in a heap. Tears came again.

As if they would never stop.

Tears, tears, tears, it seemed that was all she was capable of. Crying at night, at noon, in the morning, at mealtime.

Tears. Unending tears.

Arthur had banished her to her room until she could stop. "Seeing you weep demoralizes the men. You need to be strong. You need to rise to the occasion and be the princess they need."

The people come first . . . they do . . . but everything hurts, to breathe, to eat . . . I can't do this much longer. It doesn't make any sense to me. Why does everything hurt? It even hurts to cry.

Essie had not shed a tear.

She was in shock.

Arthur had swung into this war and stepped into his new position as king without a faltering step and now they were at Raven Castle.

The stronghold of the true and rightful king of Chambria's kings and queens.

A castle fortress since Chambria was birthed as a nation. It once had been the capital, until the new one was laid at the heart of Chambria's land. As long as they remained here, they would be proclaimed the rightful king and heirs of Chambria, that would not be contested. Raven Castle was unreachable by a force of the enemy from either Belterra or the Lord Chancellor and his evil men without massive losses.

Raven Castle was safe.

It was said that whoever held Raven Castle, held the kingdom of Chambria and it would never slip from their grasp into the hands of others.

Many hands had tried to take Chambria into their own since it had been birthed and crowned a kingdom.

Perhaps because Chambria had once been the beating heart of the great Lands of Avonelle, from which the king ruled, that the people kept trying to destroy and corrupt its core.

Chambria, the richest land hemmed in by caldera born mountains that guarded her borders like sentinels, with few gaps to allow anyone in. But it was not her borders that needed protecting. The world outside had learned to respect her walls, but within her borders with the mountain's backs turned to protect them from the outside world, danger boiled within, erupting in war and tragedy . . . not so unlike the legend that surrounded the creation of the countries of Avonelle.

They said once upon a time a mountain larger than any man could climb stood at the center, surrounded by smaller mountains that longed for a taste of heaven in which that mountain bathed.

Storytellers always told it as if the mountains had once been people. Telling of their jealousy, envy, and worship of the greatest mountain. The earth from below became weary of the mountains' crying and rumbling jealousy and warned if they did not stop, there would be consequences.

Of course the mountains did not listen to earth who was below, they never learned to be quiet, nor to be content to merely scrape the sky. One night, the earth lost its temper with the little mountains and shivered and shook. From its depths spurted liquid flames that covered the mountains and lands below it with scalding burns. The sky wept until it turned red and rained down ash and stone instead of water. The sun hid its bright face behind a red mask that dimmed him like the moon. When earth was done with its tantrum peace returned. There remained nothing of the mountain that scraped the heavens only a giant red hole in the ground, that turned to black stone, and from black stone the years eventually turned it into fertile soil. The mountains around the caldera fell silent, turned their back, and became stone, never again lifting up their voices to protest their position or any of the mountains around them lest they be destroyed as was the great mountain.

From then on there were different legends of who had been the first rightful king over all of the people of Avonelle. Some claimed he was born in Belterra, others said Falway, some legends said he was born from the scalding liquid that came forth from the earth—but that was just preposterous. Man had been created long before that from the dust of the earth by the only true God, and woman came from the side of the first man—to be by his side so that they may lean on one another.

That is another thing.

The Lord Chancellor is demanding my hand in marriage! How dare he? Arthur is soundly refusing, of course, but instead he wants me to craft an alliance with the only country who has any sort of access to Chambria. That stupid fissure in the mountains. Falway.

A chill ran down her spine.

I don't think I can love again. The hands that killed Richard belonged to my betrothed. How can I ever trust anyone ever again? A shudder ran through her. *If I cannot trust the man who vowed to love and protect me—how can I trust any man but my brother? But even he—if he would only understand . . .*

There was a gentle rap on her door. It was the pattern of Essie's knock.

"Come in," she said, scrambling from the floor.

The door opened and Essie entered, mute.

She had not cried, nor spoken a word since the accident. Only her eyes spoke; they were large and brown, like their mother's with her golden-brown hair—while Regina and Richard had taken after their father's side of the family, raven hair, and eyes the color of the sky.

Essie came to her, slipping her arms around her waist, pressing her head against Regina.

"Are you afraid?"

Essie shook her head.

"Sad? Won't you cry, dearest?" she whispered softly.

There was another shake.

Leaning down, Regina pressed a kiss to the top of her sister's head.

"Essie . . . it would help you."

There was a vigorous shake of her head.

Seven years were between them. There had been other babies born between them, but she barely remembered them—they hadn't lived longer than the day they were born—but Essie she remembered. Entering their mother's chambers on tiptoe in her best dress to see the new baby, she had been greeted by an unexpected wail from a strong set of lungs that had startled her into spinning backwards into a laughing Arthur's chest.

"I was just your age when you were born, and you greeted me the same way. What goes around comes around."

Richard had been the first to hold her; she had been too in awe and slightly frightened of the loud red-faced bundle to think of holding her. Richard, who'd had the chicken pox at Regina's birth and been forbidden from going near her or his mother until long after his illness passed, relished the opportunity to cradle this baby sister first.

He had been so gentle with Essie, then with Arthur's arms cradled beneath her own he had placed Essie into their arms. The tiny bundle squirmed and opened her eyes, staring up at them . . . and Regina had fallen in love with Essie at that moment.

Drifting from her memories back to the present moment, she stroked Essie's hair gently back, swaying slightly and humming the tune of Chambria's lullaby.

Goodnight, my child, don't make a sound.
God is nigh thee and all that love thee are 'round
Sleep, my treasure, sleep, close thine eyes.
When you wake the morn' the sun will rise.
Stars shine bright above thee, shedding light
There is no need to fear the darkness of the night.
Mountains to guard thee, stars to keep thee
Night to renew thee, light to shine and warm thee.
Sleep, sleep, don't make a sound,
All that love thee, are thee around.

Essie shook her head, and freed herself from the embrace. Going to the window, she looked over it and down the mountain's steep ravine.

The darkening sky had slipped from blue to violet, streaks of golden apricot colored clouds strung across the sky. She sat on the wide window ledge and looked at Essie's blank brown eyes that reflected the darkening silhouette of the world before them.

"Essie, what's wrong?"

Her brown speechless eyes turned to her with a look that spoke of anger, fear, and sorrow.

"You miss Mother and Father, don't you?"

She nodded.

"And Richard?"

The tears that had not yet fallen from Essie's eyes started to swell.

"I miss them too," she whispered.

"Then—why!" Essie broke the silence of nearly two weeks with a hoarse scream.

She wrapped her arms around Essie as the tears finally came. Wishing she had the words to tell her, wishing she had the answers, wishing—wishing that she could make the world go back to where it all went wrong and start over again, so that people wouldn't hurt like this.

She was too young to understand all of this, for this to be happening, for it to be crumbling at her feet, she felt too young and unable to bear it—so how on earth had Essie held it in for so long?

"And now—I am going to lose you too!"

"No! You're not, you're never going to lose me at all. I'll be here for you always."

"Arthur—he said—he said—I heard him say that man from Falway . . ."

"No, my darling, I'll never let a man from Falway take me away."

"But the messenger said . . ."

"Messenger? He's been able to get messengers through to Falway?"

"Birds, he's been sending birds."

"No! No!"

"He said tonight . . ."

Fear and rage tumbled through her, knocking at her knees and pumping her heart so loud she could hear it in her ears.

"Where is he?"

"The courtyard with that—that man."

"Prince Eric?"

"No—I don't know . . . he's all in black."

"No." Regina flew to her feet and through the corridors until she reached the balcony that looked down on the courtyard.

A man all in black with a black horse stood talking with her brother, a sword at his back, his side with sheaths of daggers around his belt. He looked like a traveling armory.

I will not go with him.

Sweeping down the stairs, she crossed the courtyard towards her brother.

"Regina?" His voice sounded surprised, and not pleased.

"When were you going to tell me?"

"In a few minutes."

"You can't do this, Arthur, you can't just bundle me off to Falway like a piece of unwanted baggage."

"Who told you?"

"Essie, and it's breaking her heart!"

"Essie? She spoke?" He lurched towards the stairs as if to go to their little sister, then stopped, looking down at her.

"It's too late. I've made the treaty with the king of Falway. Once you're married, he'll send his army. He's just come back from a war. We have to give them something; an alliance is all we have."

"We have gold, we can pay his army, we can pay men from Belterra, you can hire this man . . ."

"The money is in the treasury. We have none here on this mountain. It's a stronghold of safety, not a treasury . . ."

"Think of me, Arthur! I can't bear to leave you or Essie . . ."

"I am thinking of you! I have been doing nothing else but thinking of you and Essie. Now stop thinking about just yourself for one moment and listen to what I am telling you."

His voice dropped and he hissed out between his teeth, "I am thinking of you, of the people, of Essie—if you want a future, any future at all and don't want to be murdered in your bed—you will go with this man . . ."

"Arthur." She gripped his arm, and he flinched—barely. "I am sorry, but please don't make me go. I don't want to leave you, or Essie or Chambria. If I leave—I can never come back."

"And what would you stay here for? Father, Mother, and Richard's funeral? Your betrothed who has betrayed us? There is nothing here for you, Regina."

"There is you, there is Essie."

"And there is our people. Regina, what our country needs right now, is Falway's help, and you can get that. I cannot and Essie can't. But *you* can . . ."

"Arthur, please."

He looked down at her, his brown eyes firm.

"Arthur," she pleaded; pleading had always melted Richard's heart to bend to her will or at least to a mutual agreed understanding, but Arthur seemed only to harden with a shake of his head.

"As your king"—he swallowed, his Adam's apple bobbing in his throat—"I command you to go to Falway and marry Prince Eric."

Regina felt as if the last of her life was extinguished from her lungs. She blinked twice, trying to understand and take in his words fully and completely. "Arthur," she whispered.

"I command"—his brown eyes burned into hers, his unbending will, every muscle in his face tensed, jaw clenched—"what our parents would want. What is right for the people; we were born to serve them and not ourselves, or have you forgotten that?"

"Yes, my king," she whispered, releasing her hand from his arm. He was no longer her brother; he was her king. Arthur as she had known him all her life was gone. "I will do as you say. For . . . our people."

"Thank you," he whispered, then raised his voice to a commanding tone. "Prepare to leave at once."

"At once?"

"We will leave under the cover of dark," said the man for the first time, his dark blue eyes flashing to meet hers, and she took a moment to study him—as it was obvious he had been studying her. His hair was parted to the side, a stray forelock falling across his brow. He looked as if he hadn't shaved in a few days, emphasizing his trimmed sideburns. His posture spoke of someone who was at ease; royalty was nothing new to him. Nearly crying her heart out didn't move him—his body and soul seemed chiseled out of stone.

She looked up at Arthur, his brown eyes meeting hers. *Don't send me with him—please . . .* but Arthur's eyes too were set in determination.

"I'll go get ready."

"Make sure you eat and get some rest. We'll wait until it's fully dark; you have nearly two hours before we leave," said the man with the flashing blue eyes.

"Thank you." And turning, she left the courtyard and rushed back to her rooms.

Oh, Essie . . .

THREE

In the forest leading up to Raven Castle, he realized he was not alone. Eyes were watching from behind trees, and they were not friendly ones.

Spies.

He acted as casual as he had been trained, listening for the shaft of a nocked arrow to be sent whistling in his direction, the eager footsteps of a man slipping up on his prey, the groan of a branch overhead as someone prepared to jump him.

But none of these came. No one knew why a man of Falway would be traveling through the Chambrian forest—true, he could be going to Raven Castle, but he could just as well be weaving his way down to the capital to offer his assistance.

He took a turn towards Raven Castle, dismounting, his horse now a guard for his back as he made his way towards the door.

"Announce yourself."

"A messenger from Falway."

The door swung open, and he stepped in.

A steward was there to greet him with a slight bow.

"The king is expecting you—if you'll just step this way."

A man stood in the courtyard waiting for him. *This can't be good. If this is the most private place he can speak to me.*

"You're from Falway?" challenged the young king, his eyes sweeping over him, assessing him.

"King Fredric sent me."

"Good, you've come just in time." Though there was nothing in body language that said he was frightened, his eyes betrayed him. Eliot glanced around the courtyard. Men had gathered; Eliot looked at each one of them in the dwindling twilight. The young king had a right to fear, these men might be his side—but they weren't all his. Several of them Eliot wouldn't have trusted just by looking at them, and he could tell the young king knew it too.

"I haven't told my sister of your arrival yet or of the plans I've been making with Falway. She has been dis-traught as you can imagine over the loss of our parents and brother—her betrothed was among the ones who betrayed us. She is rather . . ."

"Emotional?"

"Yes."

"Can she control herself? There were men in the forest. Spies . . ."

"Will it be safe?"

"It will be if she is ready to leave when I say."

"You are my only hope, you realize."

"I understand completely. We will move soon."

"Tonight," put in the young king.

"Yes, tonight."

He caught sight of movement by the rail above the courtyard. A young woman flew down the stairs and across the courtyard, her black hair flowing behind her and her blue eyes sparkling with rage, despite their puffy, reddened state. There were flushed flames of red on her pale thin cheeks.

He was struck by how she carried herself: like a queen despite her clear distress.

This must be the sister. He's got a war on his hands . . .

"Here she comes," Eliot warned.

The young king turned in time to face her as she came up to him.

"Regina?"

"When were you going to tell me?" she spat out in betrayed anger.

"In a few minutes," he countered gently.

"You can't do this, Arthur, you can't just bundle me off to Falway like a piece of unwanted baggage."

"Who told you?" Anger flickered in his eyes as he scanned his men to see who had betrayed them, causing this division and public scene.

"Essie, and it's breaking her heart!"

"Essie? She spoke?" He lurched away and then turned his full attention back to his sister, with a steel entering his shoulders and working its way through his frame. "It's too late. I have made the treaty with the king of Falway. Once you're married, he'll send his army."

The girl was wounded, she almost wasn't rational—she had a head on her shoulders, but it wasn't in good use, pain had overridden her senses and her dignity. She wanted to cling to what she loved and what she knew above everything else—she wanted to hold the last threads of her world together, not realizing as she held on to them, they were unraveling further. *The hardest thing to do when you are losing something is to let go.*

Then King Arthur snapped one of her threads from her grasp.

"I command!" he said, pausing as the words hit her squarely to her heart.

Eliot saw the shock of his words run through her.

The young king pushed forward, reasoning with her, trying to gentle the blow he had dealt but still hold his ground. "What would our parents want? What is right for the people—we were born to serve them and not ourselves, or have you forgotten that?"

"Yes, my king, I will do as you say. For . . . our people." She released her grasp on him and stepped away as if she had been burned.

"Thank you, prepare to leave at once."

"At once?" The words sent a shock wringing through her again.

"We will leave under the cover of dark," said Eliot, for the first time speaking in her presence. It was best to establish his position as her next guardian, while she was still in a listening mood.

She studied him for a moment before turning back to her brother with a pleading in her eyes that was denied.

"I'll go get ready."

"Eat and get some rest. We'll wait until it's fully dark; you have nearly two hours before we leave," Eliot directed.

"Thank you," she murmured to him before leaving the courtyard and rushing back to her quarters.

"Can I have refreshment for my horse and myself?"

"At once," acquiesced the young king.

"And a private audience with you in my chamber."

"I will arrange it. Refreshment for our guest and his horse, at once! Willis, show our guest to his private chamber. You, stable boy, refresh his horse."

"Feed him only grains," Eliot told the stable boy as he took his saddlebag down.

Water for refreshing himself was brought with a generous plate of food.

Opening his pack, he took out his spare change of clothing, and the bundle meant for the princess. An all-black dress and cape.

Quickly he refreshed himself and changed clothing, while he ate.

"You clean up nicely?"

"Falway regulations: besides, I am sure your sister doesn't want to be seated behind a man who's been riding and sweating in the saddle for two days." He shrugged. "Not that she won't smell like that by the time we get to Falway, but we can at least start her off gently."

"How long will it take you to get to Falway?"

"Two to three days."

"And the men?"

"The wedding should happen within twenty-four hours of her arrival and the men should be underway through the pass at once."

"Five days at the very least then?"

"Send the king word, urge for assistance at once now that I am underway, by Eliot's suggestion."

"I can put your name to it?"

"The king is good about trusting his men."

"I shall."

"I don't like to do this to you. But I am taking your sister within the half-hour."

"Half-hour?"

"I said two hours in the courtyard . . ."

"You don't trust them?"

"No."

"Neither do I."

"You can come with us; you don't need to hold this place to battle for your throne."

"But you don't understand. Raven Castle is the stronghold of the rightful heir. If I abandon it, my people will abandon me as well. I can't leave them or this place."

"And your men can't hold it for you?"

The young king shook his head.

"Your youngest sister?"

"I keep Essie with me . . . I don't know but there needs to be a line of succession within Chambria, if anything should happen."

"Your sister and I will leave by the back door, then I suggest you firmly and securely block the entrance from any further use."

The young king started. "You know about the back gate?"

"I am from Falway, we know everything—or almost. Your men can't know when she's leaving exactly and the path from the back gate will keep us hidden until we are halfway down the mountain and nearly to Belterra."

"Right."

"Can you take this to your sister? I'll go to her once my horse is ready."

"There is a secret passage from the stable . . ."

"Third stone to the left."

"Falway really does know everything."

"Only to protect."

"And for that, I am grateful. I'll take this to my sister immediately. She will be ready."

"Don't tell her though—we don't want another scene on our hands with the risk that your lords might overhear it."

"Agreed."

The young king turned to leave, then at the door turned once again. "Thank you for this."

"It is my honor. A word of advice if I may . . ."

"Please."

"If you value your life, you'll kill the lord in the red doublet with silver trimmings. He had dark hair and stood at the bottom of the stairs when I entered."

"Kill?" quivered the young king's voice.

"If you value your life and that of your sister."

"Thank you." And the door closed.

FOUR

She clung to Essie tightly, trying to comfort her sister and herself as she tried to face her new future.

"I don't want you to go."

"I don't want to go either . . . but I must."

"Can't you tell him you won't go?"

"I tried—and he commanded me to go . . ." It was hard to say those words; he had broken part of her trust in him with those words. He had not convinced or reasoned with her, just commanded. *But shouldn't I trust him enough to do what he wishes—why does it hurt?*

Arthur entered, a bundle of black under one arm and a tray of food in the other.

"Regina, I need you to put these on at once, and get something to eat. Essie and I will help you pack what you need."

"There is nothing to pack," she said quietly.

"Of course," he said with a glance downward. They had brought nothing with them from the valley, and she had only managed to keep decent by washing this dress nearly every night. Spare clothes for the men had been found but not for her and Essie.

"Essie," said Arthur, holding out his arms to her.

The girl released her and ran across the room to him, wrapping her arms around him tightly. He dropped a kiss on her forehead and whispered something in her ear.

"Don't make her go."

"I am sorry, darling, I don't want to . . . but we must, all of us must be brave. Can you do that, Essie, can you be brave with Regina and I?"

Essie lifted her head high and nodded. "I will." Her voice trembled.

"Now, I need a moment with Regina, and then I will come to you."

Essie slipped out the door, and Arthur turned to Regina. "He's sent you these," he said, offering her the bundle of clothing. "And I have brought you this," he said, offering her the tray of food.

"I am not that hungry."

"He said to prepare to leave, eat and rest if you can, please."

"I will do my best."

"If there was another way to do this—you know I would."

"I understand," she answered, though her heart still rankled with the reasoning of it all.

"I am sorry, Regina."

"Me too," she said. "So sorry, I shouldn't have acted the way I did."

"You were afraid—" He opened his arms to her, and she rushed into them. She had learned one thing. Life was too short to keep grudges, to hold out hate over those you love.

He pressed a kiss into her hair. "We both were," she heard him whisper.

"What?"

"Nothing," he answered. "Now get ready to go, so you can get some rest. Essie will be back to say goodnight in a few minutes, and then I want you to rest."

"So soon?"

"Yes, soon."

"All right."

Arthur left, closing and locking the door behind him. Changing quickly, she washed herself before putting on the new black linen dress.

At least it's the right color for mourning. My other dress . . . She glanced at it, the regal colors, and stubborn blood stains that mocked her still. Sitting down, she nibbled on the bread and cheese that Arthur had brought in. A moment later there was a knock at the door.

"Arthur and Essie,"

"Come in!" she invited and the door swung open with both entering with somber faces.

Essie ran into her arms. "I am going to miss you so much. So, so much."

"And I you, with every breath I take."

She looked up and at Arthur who strode across the room and took them both in his arms.

"Have you eaten?"

"I was just starting."

"Should we join you?"

"Yes."

They sat together on the floor, Arthur toasting the bread over the fire. Their meal was brief and somber, a sad smile here, a look there and then it was over.

"He said you should rest—you'll be up most of the night riding, so Essie and I will leave you to get some sleep."

"I don't feel a bit tired."

"Well, at least lie on your bed just for a little while. I'll feel better knowing you rested at least a little bit."

"I will try."

"Come, Essie," he said, taking her hand.

"Good night, Regina!" said Essie quietly.

"Good night, Essie, good night, Arthur."

"Good night, Regina." And they left, the door slightly open.

Getting to her feet, Regina gathered the wool cloak in her arms; she would use it as a blanket instead of disturbing the blankets on the bed. She looked at the room around her. *This is the last time I will be here. The last time that I will call Chambria my home. Oh, I don't want to leave—I don't want to leave at all.* She looked around the room, recalling the last memories she had of their family coming up here for a summer visit to escape the heat of the city. They had sat before that very fire playing games together.

Mother and father had entered and sat on the chairs on either side of the fireplace.

They laughed together.

And it was all extinguished in a nightmarish moment.

They would never come back.

There would be no more summers with her family.

They were gone.

How can life change so quickly? How can something you love so dearly be taken away before you even know you're losing it? How can one you trust take advantage of you cruelly?

At that moment a hand slipped over her mouth, and she tried to scream but it never left her lips.

The door to the princess's room was open. She stood in the middle of the floor staring at the fire as if transfixed. She was wearing the black dress, and the black cloak was in her hand.

He slipped inside, closing the door silently behind him. She didn't move, she hadn't heard his near silent feet above the crackle and pop of the fire in the grate casting her shadow long and black across the room like a haunting shadow of predator creeping upon prey. She hadn't sensed his new and unknown presence in the room. He slipped behind her and placed a hand over her mouth. She jumped, her cry of alarm never slipping past her lips. As she struggled, he slipped his arm around her and dropped his lips to her ear.

"It is I, Eliot of Falway, I've come to fetch you. I need you to be silent. Do not fight me and I will release you. We need to go."

She wriggled in his grasp.

"I need your word that you won't fight me."

Her body stilled. There was a slow nod.

"Keep your voice low, we don't want anyone to hear us."

He released her and she spun around to face him, eyes flashing, cheeks still damp with tears. "You said I had two hours."

"That is what I wanted your lords to think . . . we leave at once; it is dark enough. The sooner we are in Belterra and then Falway the better. Your Lord Chancellor has no treaty with the king of Belterra. Any of his men coming after us armed would be seen as a declaration of war on Belterra, and once in Falway, you'll be very safe."

"But now?"

"Now."

Her eyes searched his face. "The lords, you don't trust them?"

Eliot's mouth twitched. "I don't trust many people, especially in a country that is divided, and as your brother mentioned the Lord Chancellor does have all of the money at his disposal, as well as lands of the nobles he killed and which he can now divvy up to those who serve him or his purposes well."

Her lips quivered.

"But we are . . . they swore their loyalty to my father."

"A man in war thinks first for himself, and then for others. If there is family, debts, or pride at stake, you must be very careful of any man for you never know what he may do. Now come, the night is wasting, and we'll need every black inch of it. Don't say a word, not a single syllable, put on your cloak and follow me."

She swept the cloak around her shoulders, fastening the clasp at her throat. Eliot led her out of her room, down a hallway, then another, until they came to the storage room where another hidden doorway would lead to where he had his horse waiting for them. Turning to her, he pressed his finger to his lips in a warning reminder. His gloved hands ran along a stone, searching for one that would yield beneath his touch; he found it and pushed. The door swung open, and he heard a tiny gasp behind him. Turning, he saw her wide eyes, jaw slackened in awe.

He motioned her forward with his hand, offering it to her as they came to a wooden staircase. Clinging to his hand, she stepped in; he followed, closing the door behind them.

"Can I speak now?" she whispered.

"Quietly," he cautioned.

"Where are we?"

"Going under the castle to the back passage out."

"Back passage out?"

"Yes, it's along the mountain and very steep."

"How come I never knew?"

Eliot shrugged in the dark, leading her down the stairs. "Come."

Soon they arrived at the bottom of the staircase where his horse was waiting patiently.

"You're going to ride, and I am going to lead him, at least until the path is wider."

"Does my brother—I didn't really get the chance to say goodbye—just good night."

"Regina!" came the young king's breathless voice from the other passage.

"Arthur?"

There were quick footsteps, and a moment later the young king was standing before his sister. For a long moment neither said a word.

"Mother and Father would be so proud of you, and the woman you have become. I am sorry I won't be there. That you must do this alone . . ."

"It's my privilege." Eliot heard the fight in her voice to get the words out. "I'll do everything I can to make you proud."

"I know you will."

"Will you send Essie to me, for a visit?"

"For a visit, yes, of course, next summer," he said, but Eliot heard the uncertainty in his voice.

"Won't you come with us; we could all go."

"Regina—you know."

"I know. I know—I didn't mean to make it harder on you. I am proud of you as king, and as my brother."

He pulled her into an embrace, and Eliot heard the gentle words. "God bless you and keep you, Regina. I love you." Before he tore himself away from them he swung Regina into the saddle.

"Take good care of her," he charged.

"I will—always," Eliot promised.

And with that King Arthur was gone.

Eliot moved to where the stone would be that opened the door onto the slip passageway that would take them half-way to Belterra hidden from sight.

Stars shone, and the half-moon reflected his light to earth with a silver touch that frosted everything it could reach. The path was narrow, but wide enough for his horse—how safe it was for something that hadn't been well maintained in order to keep its secrecy was another matter.

SIX

The night wind blew cold gusts against her, ruffling the Falway man's hair and playing with the horse's mane; her own hair she had carefully tucked away in the hood of the cloak.

What kind of adventure is this? Life stopped feeling real at that banquet, but now it had taken a new turn. Here she was slinking out of her own country like a criminal to marry a man she had never met in a hastily formed alliance. There was none of the pomp and performance that should be accompanying her, no lady's maids, no jewelry, no Chambrian dowry that could purchase half a kingdom, the pearl necklace that queens had worn since the first Chambrian queen would not be around her neck as she said yes to the man who was to be her husband. There had been no dress fittings, no gossip in her chambers, no conversation with her mother about what wedded life was to be. *I am no longer a princess, I am a survivor.*

Arthur's last words ran through her mind, and she wished she'd had a moment to say them back to him. To tell him one last time that she loved him, loved Essie, that God would protect his reign. She closed her eyes and prayed, begging heaven for protection of her brother, Essie, and their futures, and whatever it would bring. *God—I don't know why this is happening, or why this must go on . . . but please, keep us safe. Hold us in Your hands, keep us safe . . . please. Amen.*

They traveled in silence, Eliot said nothing, and the horse too seemed to sense the need for quiet and made not a sound. The trail seemed to last forever, cold and weariness were pulling at her, chilling her despite the wool cloak. Exhaustion was tugging at her eyes, arms, and legs, she longed for her soft bed to sleep in, but the cold kept her awake with its brisk persistence. A yawn escaped her lips, and for the first time in what seemed hours, Eliot turned to look at her.

"We are almost there, princess," he muttered quietly.

She smiled at the way he addressed her. Princess, it was strangely warm and familiar—the way her closest servants had addressed her. "Will we be able to rest for a little while?"

"No, we must see if we can reach Falway by dark."

"Falway by dark?" she wailed louder than she intended.

Eliot turned to her, shooting her a warning glance as her voice carried and echoed off the mountains around them. She bit her lip.

His gloved hand once again pressed against his lips. His look even in the dark was cautioning.

They took several steps when a sound came from above them. Soil fell from the cliff's edge and onto the trail.

"There's nothin' here."

"Nothing here? Hear that? That's an echo."

The voice sent a shiver through her. She knew that voice. It was the voice of the one that had said he loved her. That had placed a ring on her finger at their betrothal . . . *Layton*. She covered her mouth with her hand, as a tremble ran through her, fear and agony twisting together. Tears rose to her eyes that she could not give voice. She swallowed hard against the swelling of tears in her throat.

"So?"

"I heard voices," Layton persisted.

"Voices? Where did they come from? There is no one here. I am telling you it was some bird."

"A bird squawking off in the middle of the night?" scoffed Layton.

"An owl killed it."

"Not what I heard."

"What did you hear?"

"I am not sure . . ."

"Then you didn't hear anything," answered the other man. They loitered for several minutes, waiting for anything.

Eliot was perfectly still and the horse seemed to be taking shallow breaths beneath her.

At last they left, and Eliot moved, leading her down the trail.

The moon had been sinking slowly; the only thing to mark time was its movement through the sky. It was just sinking behind the trees when they came to the end of the tiny secret mountain trail, and onto the mountain itself.

Eliot removed rags from his horse's hooves which he had used to muffle the sound of its passage along the stone path, then swinging up behind her, steered the horse between and under trees. The gentle murmur of sleeping whispering pines swaying in the wind above them eased her nerves. Eliot's cloak dropped slightly over her, the warmth of protection at her back. Regina felt her eyes start to drift shut. *Why is everything so tiring? I must stay awake . . .*

SEVEN

Eliot felt the weight of her slump gradually against him even as she resisted sleep. He let out a sigh of relief, grateful that she had lasted as long as she had. Falling asleep on the horse in the pass could have been a deadly error if she had fallen. Now, hopefully he could make his way through the infested woods in peace—they were taking watches—but hopefully in the darkest hour when the moon set and only the stars twinkled above them even the most watchful man would be asleep.

Eliot contemplated his charge. She was very different from the last damsel he had secured in his saddle.

She was a creature of feeling and passion—he had seen that from the moment she flew into the courtyard, anger painted in pink on her cheeks—but she also knew how to control it if she gave her mind to it. He had seen the tears drop down her cheeks silently, as they caught the silver moonlight, glistening as they fell without a sniffle.

Doubtless she had known the men who had been speaking above them by her reaction.

Now to get to Belterra without further incident, and then to Falway. Though I'll probably be turning right around with the other men to go back to Chambria.

They were near the end of the mountain trail; another furlong down the mountain and over the ridge of the nearest hill and they would be safely in Belterra, where it would not be safe for an enemy of the Chambrian crown to follow them.

"Halt in the name of the king!" boomed a voice t's owner swinging into the road before them with sword drawn. Regina stirred in his arms, stiffening at the sight of the man in their way.

"Which king?" asked Eliot slowly, having no doubt which he was for as Regina shoved herself against him.

"King Albert."

"I know, nor serve a King Albert."

"Then know him and bow the knee for he was the former Lord Chancellor to the treacherous crown."

She shivered violently; he tightened his arm around her.

"I am here to protect you," he whispered, and withdrew the long blade at his back.

"I am for King Arthur, now stand aside."

"Give her up—and we'll let you have your life."

"Let me have my life? I didn't know I owed it to you."

"Taking the property of King Albert is a treasonous offense."

"Property? She is a princess, not property. Now let us pass or pay with *your* life."

"Men!"

A handful of figures slid from behind trees, drawing their swords.

Regina turned her face into his shoulder.

"Don't worry, princess," he whispered and laid spurs to his horse's side. Drawing to a sharp halt less than a blade's length away, letting his sword swing with all the force of the horse's inertia, before the man could parry the blow it felled him. Men swarmed forward, and he swung down from the saddle, putting himself between the coming onslaught and the princess. On the ground he had the full use of the arc of his blade and could wield it without endangering the princess or his steed's ears.

They were surrounded by men with their swords drawn. Whisking a dagger from his belt he sent it flying into the nearest man, while engaging the second with his blade, waking the forest with their singing swords. The length of his sword gave him advantage as he dispatched him into the afterlife and swung it into the third man. Three left, two rushed him at once while the other lunged for the reins of his horse. Eliot cringed, knowing the princess would be unprepared for what was coming.

The horse reared, striking at the man, sending the princess tumbling from the saddle onto the ground, gasping for air. He turned his full attention back to his opponents, felling them with sword and dagger. He turned to the last man who was stalking the princess as she was trying to scramble to her feet. He flung his last dagger into the traitor and ran his sword through, pushing him away from his charge.

He sheathed his bloodstained sword and turned to her, offering her his hand.

Shaking, she placed her hands in his.

Eliot pulled the princess to her unsteady feet.

"Your Highness, are you all right?"

She stepped back as if to escape him, and was stopped by the large tree behind her. Her eyes glued to the fallen forms around them, her own trembling.

"Princess, you're safe," he whispered, touching her cheek to turn her face from death.

She tore her terrified blue eyes away from them to look up into his. They were the color of a summer blue sky. A stray strand of her raven-black hair clung to her cheek. He wanted to tuck it behind her ear, assure her that she was safe, pull her close . . .

Eliot felt *it* strike his heart, sparking outwards.

Shooting through him like a burning arrow, throbbing in his veins.

*Of all the unreasonable times and places. And of all peo-
ple, a princess betrothed to my prince . . . you're just tired,
Eliot, keep moving.*

A Falway man always knows when he falls in love—it is
the first time he wants to kiss a girl.

He closed his eyes and gritted his teeth, trying to gather
his senses and shake the feeling that clenched his heart.

"Are you hurt?" she whispered, her hand closing around
his.

Not in that way . . . "No," he answered.

"You look like you're in pain."

"I am fine."

She breathed a sigh of relief.

There was the sound of an arrow whizzing through the air.
Eliot pulled the princess to the ground. There was the thud of
something lifeless falling through branches and to the ground.

Eliot's hand went to his sword hilt then he caught sight
of who was coming towards them in the pale morning
light. Archers advanced, surrounding them, arrows nocked,
ready to be pulled back and fired at a moment's notice. Eliot
was relieved to see the Belterrian colors.

"What was that?" Regina asked.

"We are safe, princess," he whispered, rising to his feet,
and helping her once again.

"Are you well?" asked the captain of the small company,
stepping forward.

"Yes, we are," said Eliot, guiding the princess to his horse,
and standing between her and the men—even if they were
in friendly colors.

"Good, the king mentioned what happened—said we were to lend aid if we saw you."

"You're a little far from camp, aren't you?"

"We were disbanded yesterday and we are on our way home."

"A bit far from home still, this deep in the mountains."

The captain shrugged.

Eliot couldn't help but smile. They weren't under royal orders, they came of their own will, to offer protection.

"Now let's get off this mountain before they see this as an act of war," said the captain. "We've got a camp at the base. You can refresh yourselves there."

Princess Regina still looked at them fearfully.

He dropped his voice so only she would hear. "Belterra's men, they will be good to us."

There was a sigh of relief from her lips.

"Do you want to ride or walk?"

She hesitated and Eliot chose for her, sweeping her up into the saddle. He then swung up behind her, and set his horse into a gentle walk.

"Captain, would you mind having the men gather my weapons. The sooner . . ." He let his words dangle with meaning.

"Of course." The captain turned to give orders to his men as Eliot started down the trail with his horse.

She was trembling in his arms. It was slight but he still felt it.

"You are safe, princess," he whispered reassuringly.

"I know," she whispered.

"Are you cold?"

"No, I—I don't know—I just can't stop shaking."

"Have you slept at all well since?"

"I—I have nightmares."

Of course. He tightened his arms around her. "You're exhausted, princess. You just need rest."

"Is—is that all?"

Security, reassurance . . . and love would help a great deal. "Yes, princess," he answered aloud. "Rest will help you a great deal."

Her head came to rest against his shoulder, and he winced internally.

A whimper escaped her lips.

You need a solid cry—but not here, not now. His hand brushed her arm comfortingly.

"Shh, princess." He tried to comfort. "Not here. Soon."

She turned more deeply into his shoulder.

At last they entered the Belterrian makeshift camp, with a few tents scattered and a tidy fire. The captain came to his side and Eliot turned to him. "Is there a tent where the princess can refresh herself?"

"She may have my tent," he said, leading the way to the largest canvas in the group.

Swinging down from the horse, he turned to Princess Regina, offering his assistance. She slid into his arms, drooping against him like a wilted flower. Wrapping his arm protectively around her, he opened the tent, briefly examining the small canvas home. A cot, a field table and stool. "Rest in here, I'll bring you some food soon."

"Thank you." Her voice choked on emotion.

He nodded in response and closed the tent flap behind her. He had reclaimed his weapons from the men, placing the daggers back into their place. They offered them a ration of breakfast consisting of freshly roasted meat and flat bread. First he brought a plate of hot food to the captain's tent and requested entrance.

There was no response.

Eliot swept open the flap.

Princess Regina was sound asleep on the captain's cot, not even her legs were swept up on the smooth surface. She had sat down, lowered her head, and fallen asleep. Eliot let out a sigh of relief . . . it had only been a few days ago when Lord Raburn had entered their camp and nearly destroyed another damsel.

There was no enemy here, exhaustion had overtaken her. He stood for a moment weighing his choices. Tired as he was, he could still go. He was trained for the hardness of battles, the deprivation by the necessity of king and country—but a princess flung from the richness of life into the throes of the hunted, and into the nightmares of the haunted could barely survive it.

He withdrew and turned to the captain. "She is sleeping."

"Exhausted, poor thing."

"But I cannot risk the time that it would take for her to fully recover."

"A carriage?"

"It would slow us down considerably, and I need her in Falway as soon as possible."

"So, you can't stay here and wait for her to rest?"

"No, the situation at Raven Castle is dire."

"Dire?"

Eliot nodded. "Now, if you'll lend me a fresh horse, I'll leave with her at once."

"None of ours are Falway trained."

"I know, but I need to go, and I need a good beast to get there on. I've nearly run this one to the ground, the good boy."

"I'll have it done immediately. Eat and the horse should be ready with a day's rations."

Eliot ate what he had been ready to offer the princess. As he chewed the last bite of bread, a sable steed was brought to him. Going into the captain's tent, he gathered the sleeping princess into his arms, passing her gingerly to the captain as he mounted, then leaning down, he gathered her once again in his arms, careful with how he settled her in the saddle before him.

Taking the reins, Eliot turned towards Falway.

EIGHT

Why is everything so sore? Why am I so tired? No nightmares—the first night with no nightmares . . . since . . .

A shiver ran through her. She didn't want to finish that thought. Everything was in constant motion, so much movement it hurt, everything was sore, her arms, back, legs, especially where she had landed on the ground hard when the horse had reared.

Where am I?

Opening her eyes, she glanced up to see Eliot's chin directly in front of her face, her head resting on her shoulder. He leaned slightly away.

"Awake, princess?" he asked in his deep voice.

"Yes, how long have I been sleeping?" she asked, looking at the sky; it was pale and dusky, like it had been when she had entered the captain's tent—she had been too tired to even cry before her head touched the cot's rough surface.

"All day," he answered flatly.

"What?" A blush rushed up her neck, onto her cheeks, and peaked in her ears.

There was a smirk on his lips. "You were exhausted, princess."

"All day though . . ." She shifted uncomfortably in his arms, trying to right herself into a proper riding position, but it wasn't easy to manage, especially when pain rippled through her body with echoing aches of stiffness.

"You've hardly slept in over a week I am guessing; your body saw the chance to rest and took it."

She shook her head, an uncomfortable heat crawling up her neck and into her cheeks.

"How much longer?" *The sooner I am not in his arms or maybe even his company, the better I will be—won't I? If he was a courtier I would simply order him to walk away but I can't do that here . . . and I am not sure I really want to.*

Another flush ran up her cheeks, as her heart seemed to skip a beat and she studiously scanned the scenery around them.

"Not much, we are nearly there."

"Good, because I am sore all over," she answered, trying to be sharp and put some sort of distance between them.

"I am sorry that my horse unseated you so unceremoniously, he's trained to rear like that when someone attempts to grab his reins."

"How convenient, and very painful."

"It's a military tactic. Sorry I didn't have time to warn you. Do you ride horses often?"

"Ones that are gentled for a princess to ride, yes. The wild beasts you keep taking me on, no."

There was a low chuckle from him, and he shifted slightly.

He's probably as sore as I am—if not worse. We've been riding all day and I've done nothing but sleep in his arms. Looking down at her black dress, she fiddled with the dark folds now creased with brown dirt. *My face is probably filthy—oh for a warm bath, and a new dress before I see the king and the prince of Falway. But I don't think that is to be thought of. I hope they won't take me to the altar looking like this, for a bride to be wed looking like this . . .* She cringed. *No, they won't take me like this . . . will they?*

"What has you so silent, princess?"

"Will I have time to refresh myself before—before . . ."

"I assume you will. But I am a man of duty, not details. I couldn't tell you for sure, but I am sure the king or someone will have thought of that detail so no worries."

"Why did you want to know?"

"Just making sure none of the nightmares had followed into your consciousness." His tone dropped to a whisper;

the depth and gentleness in his voice said that he knew what it was to have nightmares.

Eliot pulled the horse up on the brow of the hill they had been climbing. "Look, princess," he said.

The sight below her took away her breath.

Chambria was beautiful, but Falway?

Falway was *gorgeous*.

The castle was set on a high hill, waving its colors boldly in the tint of the waning sunlight. It was surrounded by a thriving city hedged in by large stone walls. Farms that looked like the patchwork of a peasant quilt spread southward and west; the sea lay to the north, splashing foaming white and aqua waves at a sand shore that stretched its tan arms to embrace the sea spreading as far as the western mountains.

"I thought you said we'd be arriving soon. It's still so far away."

"Closer than we were; an hour's good ride should see us there."

"An hour?"

"Yes."

"Can I get down and stretch my legs?"

"I don't see why not; the horse could use a break and drink as well." He motioned to the stream near at hand and nudged the horse off the road. He swung down from the saddle and turned to help her down.

She landed on her feet, and quickly crumpled.

"What is it? Are you hurt?"

"No, I am just so stiff and sore and everything hurts."

"I am sorry, Your Highness, the journey has not been easy on you."

Tears came sharply into her eyes. *Not now, don't cry.* She hadn't gotten the chance earlier, and now didn't seem like a better time.

Eliot's arm slipped around her. Supporting her, he led her and his horse towards the grass and the stream near the road. "Why don't you sit down for a little bit and rest up, while I take care of my horse."

He set her down in the long grass and brought his horse to the stream, removing the bit so the horse could drink freely. She extended her body out in the long grass, the luxury of release from what had been hours in one position painful and glorious all in one moment. She was sore in every joint and bone—*I feel like an old lady.*

Regina sat up when Eliot walked over to her while the horse drank deeply and handed her a canteen of fresh cold water.

"Your first taste of Falway water, Your Highness."

She drank deeply from the canteen. Water had never tasted so sweet or refreshing in her life. Next, he handed her a small flat of bread and cheese from the saddlebag.

"Sorry I don't have better to offer you. But it will have to do until you can feast from the king's table."

Bread and cheese. Her memory shot back to what felt like hours and yet years ago, she, Essie, and Arthur sitting by the fire eating this same thing, though this was certainly not toasted by a fire.

Taking a small bite, she found that the flavors were distinctly not Chambrian, but there was still the flavor of home and happiness in them. When they disappeared, Eliot moved into action once again, bridling the horse and checking the saddle girth before offering her his hand.

Inwardly she moaned.

"Sooner we get going, the sooner we arrive."

"How are you not crippled from all the riding you've been doing?" she asked, taking his hand.

He laughed, lifting her from the ground. "This is what I do for my living, I ride, I guard, I kill for my king and my country."

Kill. That word sent a shiver down her spine. She had seen firsthand how adept he was at taking the lives of others when he needed to. So far it had always been in her defense but what if he was to turn against her? She tried to shake that thought away as she looked up into his blue eyes. They were a calculating sort of blue, they were not the deathly cold ice blue, nor the deep friendly twinkling blue that invited confidences; they were somewhere between.

Without a word or warning he swung her into the saddle and mounted behind her, pushing them into motion. Down the sloping hill, across the fields, and into the city walls that seemed as high as they were thick with a triple set of gates.

"It's huge. No wonder no one attacks Falway."

"It is difficult, that is for sure. The harbors freeze in the winter, the mountains are impassible. An attack would have to be made in the spring or summer, but meeting defenses such as these and winning a siege would be odds against all odds without taking in consideration for the military prowess of Falway people who have had nothing more to do all winter but expand and hone their skills. The only way Falway would ever fall would be from within, but the code of conduct is strict for king and people alike; there is very little room to stray off the right path."

"I see now why they say Falway is impenetrable."

There was a smile in Eliot's voice as he answered. "The archers can fire bows that reach outside the city walls from atop the castle. Men don't even need to be on the city walls to defend them."

"Really?"

He nodded. "The high ground allows them to carry farther and decreases loss for our men. We can turn the sky black with arrows."

"I am glad I am becoming your ally and not your enemy."

He laughed softly and turned down a street. Regina looked at the people, they seemed happy and at ease. Children who had been playing in the street stopped to wave at them. She waved back and Eliot nodded. People seemed to know who Eliot was; nods of respect were directed towards him.

"People are staring at you," Regina whispered.

"Are you sure they aren't staring at you?"

"No, they aren't. Not really—not like they could be, not the way my people stare like I am a doll in a glass case that shouldn't be touched. They look at you." She cocked her head, looking for the words that she wanted, but they weren't coming. For the first time in her life, she was unnoticed, she was eclipsed completely in the shadow of someone else. Arthur had shone like the sun in their family, Richard had been in his shadow, and she in both of theirs, but they had not eclipsed her; she still shone like a waxing moon, always visible, always somewhat in the spotlight, not even Essie was fully eclipsed . . . but here, just now she was invisible.

The safety that came with that, the protection of being in Eliot's guardianship was not lost on her, and she wanted nothing more than to curl up and remain in this small space, closing the door on the rest of the world and hiding here—in Eliot's protection.

What? Regina's reasoning caught up with her thoughts as they seemed to spiral out of control. She reined them back in. *I am just tired. A few more hours and I can rest again. Just a few more hours . . . and I shall be the future queen of this place? What will that feel like? To be shielded by those city walls—will the prince be like Eliot?*

Anxiety swept over her, turning her stomach into knots. She was going to be someone's wife . . . and eventually a mother. All these things were happening all too soon.

"You're all right, princess, you are safe here. No harm will come to you," Eliot's voice soothed, and she turned slightly to look at him.

Those blue eyes met hers once again.

"You're tense, what is bothering you?"

"Nothing," she answered shortly, turning to face forward once again.

"Fine, lie to yourself if you will, but in all my years of life there is always more to nothing that one admits."

She bit her lip and shook her head.

A soldier was walking down the street, pack in hand, sword at his side. He called out the name of a woman. In a doorway a woman appeared, her blonde hair neatly braided, wearing a patched dress and a spotless apron. She squeaked what Regina assumed was his name and launched herself into his outstretched arms that had dropped his pack the moment he saw her. He caught her, held her, and kissed her.

Regina felt a blush creep up her cheek.

She had only seen her parents kiss once in her lifetime and to see anyone doing so in the streets seemed like an outrageous act of indiscretion. Such a thing would never be done in Chambria, especially in public.

Kissing is a private affair—or should be. She peeled her eyes away, wishing the blush would retreat from her cheeks.

"He's a soldier that will go to your defense tomorrow," whispered Eliot.

"But kissing in the street," she whispered.

"Haven't heard the stories of Falway?"

"I've heard rumors, but . . . I didn't think. In Chambria we'd never behave this way. We are far more chaste in our affections towards one another, at least when it comes to such a display of affection. A kiss on the cheek perhaps . . ."

"There are many Falway legends that circle around kisses."

Regina felt her ears getting warm at the thought of it. *Will the prince expect me to be that affectionate with others around? I could never think about kissing anyone in public, not like that.* Something inside of her quivered in strange concoctions of anticipation and dread.

The castle now was in full view; it was beautiful, larger, taller, more majestic than her Chambrian home, and there was an ache. This place felt cold and distant, ominous as if it wanted to eat her whole and never surrender her.

A guard greeted Eliot at the gate. "The king is waiting to see you."

"And the princess?"

"A room is prepared for her."

"Excellent," he answered, riding in under the stone archway.

Her heart dropped in her chest as they came out in the first courtyard of the castle. It was large and beautiful, a fountain gurgling in the center. A stable hand came running to the head of Eliot's horse and took the reins. Women were making their way across the courtyard towards them, their plain clothing stating they were servants, but their eyes saying they knew who she was and that they were coming for her. Panic burst in her chest at the thought of going with strangers into these castle walls.

Eliot's leg swung around the back of the horse, at the same time he slipped an arm around her waist, dropping them both to the ground in unison, his arm supporting her and preventing a harsh jar. He was holding her close. "You are going to be all right." The horse was between them and the oncoming ladies like a screen.

Regina looked up at him, fighting the words that wanted to burst from her lips.

Don't leave me. Don't let me go. She wanted to cling to him, he was the only familiar thing in the past several hours that had been a whirlwind, and she didn't want to lose the last thing that seemed even remotely familiar that tied her to her home.

"You're trembling again. You're still tired. Go with them, they will take care of you."

His arm tightened a moment before stepping away and motioning to the stable boy. "Take him away and reward him well, he's had a rough day."

The horse that had stood like a screen from the ladies moved away and the ladies stepped forward with low curtsies.

"Your Highness, Lady Faye and her ladies will attend you. Lady Faye, this is Princess Regina."

"Thank you, Sir Eliot. Your Highness, this way if you please," said the woman with a gentle sweep of her hand, motioning for a nearby staircase. They closed around her like a shield wall of human armor.

I feel like they are going to suffocate me. She turned towards Eliot, their eyes meeting.

"Be careful with her," Eliot cautioned, his blue eyes steady.

She wanted to reach out, to have him come to her side and make her feel safe in that eclipsed feeling once again. *I can't, I have to keep going after this hour, I might never see him again. I just must keep moving. Don't cry, Regina. Don't cry . . . don't cry, you are the Princess of Chambria, you will not cry before your new people, you will not let them think that you are weak. But Eliot . . .*

NINE

Eliot didn't need any direction, he made his way through the mazelike network to the king's audience chambers.

"Thank goodness you've come," said one of the attendants, ushering him forward through a dark paneled room hung with pictorial tapestries of various Falway tales . . . that mostly involved a kiss.

The attendant motioned for him to pause while he saw if the king was ready to see him at that moment.

He was stopped in front of the tapestry which as legend had it was where kissing was invented. An arena, a princess, and of course a Falway man. He had always thought the story was stupid—until now.

The door swung open and the attendant announced, "Eliot, Your Majesty."

Eliot stepped into the opulent hearing chamber, dark wood, gilded ceiling that amplified the light of the flickering candles.

King Fredric was pacing ferociously in his chambers.

"Your Majesty?"

"You brought the princess?"

"Safe and sound."

"And now, what am I going to do with her? Can you believe it—Eric is married."

"Married?" Shock rippled through him.

"Yes, while I was away, he fell in love and married without my permission. They wanted it to be a surprise. Surprise, my foot, he didn't want me to know it was *her*. She's an all right girl I suppose but—and they have a child, or they are going to have a child, she is six months along. Whether he is king, his child, or his brother is, will be up to the council; they don't seem to be looking very favorably upon him at the moment either. Now what am I going to do about Chambria? I've had a few very choice words with my son, but I am not sure how I am going to do this. Now, if I had known, I would have taken in Princess Esmerelda, for Wulf, but they are still children, and I am not about to marry Prince Wulf to a woman six years his elder while he is still a boy of twelve, it's preposterous."

"Your Majesty, did you receive a message from Raven Castle? Any message."

"No, why?"

Eliot's stomach twisted, and a coil of premonition twisted in his stomach.

"I am afraid there might not be any king of Chambria, if you haven't heard from him."

"King?" His own king examined him with dark eyes. "Are you saying we might have the queen of Chambria?"

"I am afraid so . . . unless he was stronger and smarter than his men. The situation from what I could see was dire, and not all of his men were his. I told him to slay one—and message you at once for reinforcements."

"It's possible the bird could have been caught."

"Flying mostly over mountains with nothing in its way?" Eliot questioned.

King Fredric gave him an agonized look. "If there is to be no marriage, there is no alliance. But what do we do with a dethroned queen and a country that has turned her out? I could send my men, but to what avail? If her people in court have been killed and the army turned against her, there is nothing to go back for. There is nothing for her to go back to . . . if her family has been slain, and she has no one to rally around her and support her. We can offer her refuge at best . . ."

"But Your Majesty . . ."

"Of course, we don't know this. I will send the troops in the morning. I will keep my word and if her brother is still alive, we will renegotiate the alliance, and send her back.

Meanwhile, I want you guarding her until Faren arrives, which should be soon. The new Chambrian ambassador arrived today—and I don't like him one bit. They had it out in my court, the old ambassador and the new. They are both confined to their chambers at the moment with heavy guards, until I know what to do with them."

"As you will it, Your Majesty."

"Did you have any problems getting here?"

"The new king's men tried to kill us, but otherwise no. She's worn out and has been traumatized. She has lost everything she's known and loved without much warning."

The king winced. "Send for me when you think she can take some news. Meanwhile freshen up and then I want you and a guard command in her antechamber to keep things in check."

"Of course, Your Majesty, anything else?"

"No, you're dismissed."

Eliot left the king's chambers and took the roundabout way to the guards' ward, walking through the hall of legends, filled with tapestries, paintings, and statues that harkened to the heroes that had crafted Falway into the place it was today, and legendary weapons of kings and swordsmen that had come before. The sword of the king who had united all Avonelle under him—only to have it shattered at his death to his various members who had once upheld him. He paused beside the sword at the tapestry that depicted King Alexander and his men. He glared at the man Julian who as legend had it had poisoned King Alexander and then taken Chambria as his loot. As Chambria had been taken and forged into a nation, it seemed to remain. In treachery it had been created, and in treachery it seemed to remain. *The sins of the fathers are truly passed down on their children.*

Going to his cabinet in the guard room, he grabbed a new change of clothes before heading to the guards' bath house, to refresh himself. Upon exiting freshly changed and strapping on his weapons, he found a small troop of king's guards waiting for him.

"We've been assigned with you to guard the princess."

"Excellent, have you all eaten?"

"Yes, sir."

"Then one of you won't mind running to the kitchen while the rest of us go to the princess's chamber. The sooner we are there the better, but I have not yet eaten. Also coffee, lots of coffee."

He made his way to the princess's antechambers to wait for his next command whether it came from her lips, or that of the king's.

Reaching their destination outside of the princess's room, Eliot stretched out on one of the low long couches. He was one of the king's men—not one of the king's guards. This was certainly his privilege and he intended to take the full ten-minute nap before the food and coffee arrived. Even after the coffee arrived, he intended to sleep until summoned.

He had rested well in the camp, after Raburn and his men had been disassembled. Everyone hovering quietly about the camp wondering if Annabeth was going to survive had given him plenty of time to sleep—but two full days of riding and he needed sleep, at the very least, a nap.

Sleep deep and sweet crested over him the moment his eyes closed, but his nose announced when coffee arrived, but his ears heard no summons so sleep a little more he would.

"Eliot?"

His eyes opened and he rose in one swift movement to look down at Lady Faye.

"Yes?"

"The princess would like to speak to you."

"Of course," he said, pouring himself coffee into an earthen vessel that had been fired to give it a glossy sheen, and snatching up a morsel of food which he could chew and swallow between his bench and the doorway, trusting bringing coffee in wouldn't be a grievous offense.

He entered with a low bow, tucking his coffee cup carefully so it would not spill. The princess was sitting next to the fire, a plate of food at her disposal untouched. She made a motion for him to sit. Moving across the floor to where she indicated, he sat down and took a long sip of coffee. "Would you like me to send for the king? He has a few things he'd like to speak to you about."

Her mouth was pursed tightly, and she waved the attendants out of the room.

Eliot leaned back in the chair and swung his right ankle to the knee of his left leg, resting his shoulder heavily against the right side of the chair.

The door closed and she turned towards him.

"Eliot, what is wrong?"

"Wrong?" He sidestepped the question. "If you feel there is something wrong, you should speak to the king about it."

"Don't push it off on him, Eliot. Something is wrong. I can tell from how the ladies treat me." Her mouth pressed together, the corners pressing sharply downward.

"Would you care for coffee, princess?" he said, taking a sip of his own.

"Coffee? No . . . does Falway have chocolate? Drinking chocolate, that is."

"I am not sure. It's not something they'd give to a soldier; the upper classes might drink it."

"Never mind then," she said with a queenly wave of her hand. "Just tell me what is wrong."

"Wrong?" he asked.

"Don't lie to me, please. I've had enough people lie to me in the past few months—I need someone I can trust—please." Her lips quivered and she looked up at him with desperation.

Please should never have to fall from a princess's lips that way. Eliot leaned closer. "Princess."

"That *is* it exactly. People are treating me kindly—but not as a future princess of Falway, not as their queen—to-be. Even with giving leave for perhaps Falway manners. These ladies were kind to me, but they did not treat me royally— there is no dressmaker standing by waiting to make over a frock for my wedding or even make something suitable over . . . I am not getting married, am I?" The question bordered on rhetorical. There was a desperate note in her tone.

"Our prince made the unfortunate choice of wedding in his father's absence and not telling his father of the matter."

Regina's cheeks paled, tears coming to her eyes. "But my country? Arthur, Essie, what will become of them, without the alliance . . ." She sank deeper into her chair, covering her face with her hands.

"He will keep his word and send troops tomorrow at the break of dawn."

"Will it be soon enough?" she asked, peeking from behind her hands.

"I trust it will be, Your Highness."

"And if it is not . . . if something happens to Chambria . . . to Arthur and Essie."

He fixed her with a look.

She rose to her feet and paced about the room. "I have the worst feeling. I should never have left." Princess Regina covered her face with her hands.

Putting down his coffee, Eliot rose from his chair and crossed the room to her side. Wishing he could dismiss her feelings and fears, tell her all would be well. But he could not. He had no proof. Everything in his mind pointed to the worst-case scenario.

"Tell me it's *just* a silly feeling," she said, looking up at him, tears in her eyes.

Words felt cold on his lips. He wanted to give her the protection of those words, but they would be nothing but a betrayal of the truth. "Is that a command, princess?"

A tear slipped down her cheek as she looked at him.

"You told me not to lie to you." As he stabbed her with words, he wanted to reach out to her, to pull her close . . .

He had wondered how Ransom did not complain while he carried Annabeth back to the camp, how jealously he had guarded her in his arms. Now, he understood, he had done the same—the ride had been long and arduous, but his heart had leapt out to intertwine his heartstrings with that of the princess. *Princess, she is a princess*—he had reminded himself all afternoon—he reminded himself now, but still the ache was there. Her blue eyes were staring at him, and she was shaking her head, tears falling.

"Eliot, please tell me you've at least heard from Raven Castle."

"The king has not heard from Raven Castle."

"No, no . . ." She turned, shuddering.

"Princess, not hearing anything . . ."

She turned to him, and shook her head, bidding him to be silent.

The doors opened and a guard stepped in. "I am sorry, Your Highness, there is a messenger here whose name is Rainus, he wishes to see you and you alone."

"Let him pass! He is the steward of Raven Castle . . . let me see him."

Instinct sent Eliot's hand to the handle of the sword at his side, staying in the shadow of the princess.

The man was ushered in. His eyes darted around the room, quivering as they fell on Eliot.

"Your Majesty, I've come to tell you, to tell you . . ."

"Tell me what?" she asked, stepping towards him.

"It's King Arthur, Your—Your—Majesty."

Eliot caught the change of her title and winced.

"He bade me give you this." He offered her his closed fist, holding it high to drop something into her hands.

+ +

She held her hand out to receive it.

Glittering in the candlelight, it dropped into her open hands.

The setting of the ruby, flanked by two ravens with wings outstretched.

She never imagined the weight of the ring could be so heavy. The last place she had seen this ring was her brother's hand.

Arthur's signet ring.

Her head spun, dark dancing in her vision.

Her middle squeezed.

She could not breathe.

Time stopped.

Regina looked up at the steward, shock tingling through her veins.

"No . . ."

Things moved in slow motion.

A flash of silver was in his right hand.

A dagger was plunging towards her.

Rainus is here to assassinate me. But why—

Eliot was between them.

A scream.

It was not her own voice—or was it?

Everything felt so far away.

Guards rushed in.

She stepped around Eliot's back, and winced.

"Eliot," she whimpered.

Emotions tangled in her chest.

She struggled for air to breathe, to command mercy for the man who had just tried to slay her—but he was a traitor. Her mind tried to bend around this information.

Rainus dropped his dagger to the ground.

"Who sent you?" charged Eliot.

"The men of the Lord Chancellor, they said if I didn't bring back news of her death they were going to—kill my family." He wheezed. "I am sorry, Your Majesty," he said, sending her a sorrowful glance.

"No! No! Essie? What about Essie?"

"Kidnapped her and brought her to the Lord Chancellor."

"Raven Castle?" she whispered.

"Fallen."

"How?"

"There was an uprising when the traitors found out you'd left. They were planning to kill you all."

"No! It can't be."

"It's so, Your Majesty," he breathed raggedly.

"But Essie—what are they going to do?"

"She'll marry his son when she is of age . . ."

"No, no—she can't, she won't . . ."

"And how are you going to stop him?" asked Rainus. "Since I didn't kill you, he'll put a bounty on your head, a king's ransom dead or alive. The only place you'll be safe is locked in a tower, and then—even poison can find you there, a pillow in your sleep . . ."

"Silence!" charged Eliot, pushing his sword farther into the man, twisting the blade. "Turn! You don't need to see this, Your Majesty."

"Eliot . . . please no."

"Guards!"

"Don't kill him, please don't!"

The room paused from its whirl of movement and chaos to a silent standstill.

"Regina, he's already a dead man . . . once I relieve him of my sword . . ." He gave her a look that finished the sentence.

She glanced down at the steward. The truth was in his eyes.

I want to run . . .

Queens don't run.

I am queen. Oh, God, I can't be queen.

Guards stepped between her and Eliot and Rainus. She turned back to the widow and covered her ears. A shiver slipped up her spine.

The rightful queen of Chambria. The weight of that realization on top of everything else dropped her to the ground.

Time and life seemed to stop altogether, and yet it raced, swirling at a rate her heart could not keep up with. She couldn't breathe.

There was motion in her room but she couldn't move.

"Princess." Eliot's voice broke through the echoing screaming silence that would not cease.

She flung herself into his arms. Air returning to her lungs.

"Why!" *Is that even my own voice?* "Why?"

She had never felt so small and weak, as if the universe was trying to eat her like a howling hounding wolf.

One arm tightened around her, the other stroked her hair soothingly.

He didn't say a word, and Regina wasn't sure if she was glad that he didn't—or if she was dying to hear another voice in the savage universe.

"What am I going to do?"

"Take back your throne."

"What?" She turned her head to look up at him.

His blue eyes looked into hers. He was steadying, so firm and sure of himself. "Take. Back. *Your*. Throne." He said each word with slow deliberate cadence that she could not misunderstand even in her spinning world.

"My throne?"

He took the ring from her hand and slid it onto her left pointer finger.

She looked down at it. Something that had fit so beautifully on her brother's pinky finger seemed to swallow her hand.

"Do you want this?" he was asking her.

She looked at him. *He is speaking of the impossible.*

"Taking back your throne is the only way to not live in fear for the rest of your life."

"Essie . . ."

"If you want to protect her, *you* will take back your throne."

He was speaking of it so confidently. "How?"

"Take it back."

"Falway's army? What if I lose?"

"We don't need an army."

"We don't?"

"No."

"How?"

"You just need me, and about ten more men."

"What?"

"Do you trust me?"

She looked into his eyes; they held her gaze as no other man had ever dared to look at her. The question he asked echoed deep in his eyes, and into her heart.

"Yes. You are the only one I trust."

"Then, let's take back your throne."

TEN

Tose summer-blue eyes looked up into his and his heart jerked. But he couldn't think of that right now—a plan had been forming in his mind, and there was no time to lose.

"Men, get ready to leave."

"At once," said the commander, moving out.

"At once?" her voice echoed beside him.

He turned. "Yes, there is no time to lose." Untangling himself gently from her, he walked to the wardrobe that stood in the corner. He opened it and pulled out a cloak. Bringing it back, he swept it around her shoulders.

"The ride will be long and cold."

She was looking up at him in a daze, as if the dagger he had stopped had found its way into her heart.

Taking her hand gently, he led her to the armory. And armed himself with several more daggers, strapped on his long sword, and snatched up his ready pack. Entering the courtyard, horses were saddled and ready. Leading her to her mount, he paused.

"Princess—Your Majesty, I know you're still in shock over everything—but there is no time to lose. Riding separately."

She nodded. "I understand."

"She is Falway trained, a very gentle beast. Don't pull on her reins too hard and she won't give you any problems."

She only nodded again and looked up at him with her blue eyes, on the verge of tears again. He wanted to stop the world just for a moment and pull her close into the harbor of his arms, but not with ten men standing around him. He'd already breached far too many decorum rules to ponder breaking more without consequences following, but it would not allow him to wipe away the tears as they fell.

"May I help you mount?"

To this she nodded, reaching for him.

He stepped to her side and helped her mount and her wince did not escape him. *If my horse hadn't completely unseated her, if I had been able to warn her—but it is too late now.*

Mounting, he glanced at the formation behind him: they surrounded the queen of Chambria.

At his nod they moved forward into the bleak night.

Dawn was peeking its head over the horizon when Eliot pulled up his horse.

"We make camp here," he said, motioning into the forest. They broke from the main passageway between Chambria and Falway and wove their way through trees and over rocks to an empty cave. Dismounting, the soldiers led the horses toward the back of the cave. This was a drop-off or stopping point for Falway spies to leave information or meet with an informant.

Queen Regina looked beyond weary, as he stepped to her side, to help her dismount. Upon reaching the ground she took a small step forward and leaned into him, her head resting on his doublet, her body trembling. Exhaustion had coiled its arms around her.

"We will rest here today, Your Majesty."

She nodded and stepped back slightly, claiming his left arm for strength.

He brought her forward in the cave and spread his cloak over the stone. "Lie down and rest, you'll be surprised at how comfortable it is."

"Rock?"

"Soft as a cloud," he answered.

A faint smile pulled at her mouth and she dropped to the floor, curling up in a ball on his cloak, pulling the edges over her.

Eliot finished his inspection of the cave and checked the secret keeping stone. There was nothing new. Exactly what he expected, but not what he had hoped for.

When he turned around ten men were waiting on him for orders.

"What are we going to do here?" asked Victor, his arms crossed.

"Take back her throne."

"How?"

"Sleep for a few hours, then a few of us go in for recent information. Once I know more, I'll make my final plan."

"And that is?" put in Victor.

Eliot quirked a smile at the captain. He knew him well. There was always a main plan, variations were made on variables.

"How do you feel about collecting a king's ransom?" asked Eliot.

The men's eyebrows raised.

"It'll take me into the castle."

"And there isn't a backway that will let you in?" asked Victor.

Eliot pondered the castle plans kept in Falway's record rooms. He had studied them until they were burned into his mind years ago, and there hadn't been any updates to the castle since then.

"They know that we used it to escape Raven Castle. While I don't think they expect us to use the entries to attack, I don't feel like sneaking in only to have my throat slit. I'd rather we use the one in Chambria's capital to kidnap Princess Esmeralda into Falway's care."

"You're going for a statement with the queen," Victor answered.

"Yes, a very large one."

Victor nodded, signing on to his plan.

"Some of us will take watches, you rest up. Around noon, three of us will make our way into town, and bring you back news."

"Excellent, now I do believe it's time for a rest."

He moved back towards the entrance where Queen Regina was sleeping, and stationed himself across the entrance, leaning against the stone wall. Closing his eyes, he fell asleep.

A warm feeling wrapped around her.

Security stanched the bleeding ache in her soul.

When was the last time I felt this way? Not in a castle but on a stone floor of a cave surrounded by men I barely know.

Shifting, she sat up, sore and stiff from the solid stone beneath her, and stretched. It still felt as if every bone ached.

Eliot stirred, awakening, the sleepiness in his eyes disappearing within two blinks.

"Rest well, Your Majesty?"

The words sounded foreign.

Majesty.

There was a weight to that title she had never imagined her shoulders would carry.

Majesty, I am anything but majestic at the moment . . . oh for one of my ladies to help me look suitable.

The question in Eliot's eyes reminded her that she hadn't answered him.

"I did, as much as can be expected. Thank you."

His eyes seemed to press her with a question she couldn't quite discern, they expressed worry but hesitation lingered there . . .

He put words to it. "Nightmares." The word was barely a whisper.

She paused to think.

No nightmares. It felt strange—if anything, there should have been more. Rainus had attempted to slay her. Surely that moment would have reared its ugly head into a venomous nightmare.

Looking into his eyes, she shook her head.

He nodded slowly. "Too tired, that is a good thing."

There was an impulse to go to his side and curl up beside him to feel small and safe in the shadow of someone strong.

But princesses don't do that, a princess would never . . . a queen would never. There are so many things a queen would never do . . . How am I ever going to be and do it all?

Eliot offered her a wry smile, and she sent one back—his widened, and a blush started to creep up her neck and color her cheeks. She glanced out the cave entrance. Light was once again dwindling, into night.

"I am making a habit of sleeping through the day." She could see Eliot nod out of the corner of her eye. "You don't seem to be bothered by it . . . do you live like this often?"

"I do. I am at the call of my king and my country."

"And my country?"

"My king sent me to aid you—and that is what I am doing."

Somehow, that answer hurt.

There was no reason that it should.

I don't want to just be a duty—but why do I care that I am more than a duty to you?

A new ache thrummed with her heartbeat, and she stood up and swung her arms to loosen her tight aching muscles.

"Can I leave the cave?"

Eliot's eyebrows rose. "Two of the men are out there keeping watch. You can step out, but I wouldn't go far."

She nodded and headed towards the fresh air.

The evening air was chilled, seeming to have never fully warmed in the heat of the day. A shiver slipped down her spine. She was in a no-man's-land of sorts; the border between Chambria and Falway had never been fully established, and neither seemed willing to fight over where the border went exactly. As long as Falway didn't invade their land, and if Chambria didn't press its fighting neighbor, there was peace. All was well, but this meant she was standing exactly where she was in her life, neither in Falway or Chambria, she had a future in neither. Falway was protecting her, Chambria had a price on her head— and yet it was hers.

She ran her finger over her brother's signet ring, memorizing the detail of the raven's wings hedging in the stone. This had been his design, and he had chosen a ruby over the traditional amethyst, which was Chambria stone found in many of her mines. Gold and silver ran through the mountain's veins. Cliffs and quarries of marble, and spiked amethyst in abundance, along with the occasional glittering diamond. Chambria was littered with riches, and unparalleled black soil that made even little farms lucrative if well managed. But here, she had nothing.

She, the queen of Chambria, had nothing but eleven Falway men to protect her back, and her brother's signet ring as her claim to the throne.

Regina felt every emotion all at once, and yet she felt numb, she wanted to cry—and she also never wanted to weep again. It felt as if this was all a dream and that she should wake up any moment and hear any of the four voices that she had lost in the last two weeks—or had it been two lifetimes? She felt infinitely older and yet like the tiniest fragile babe that should be swaddled and cuddled next to her mother, protected from the raging world.

She glanced down and there bowing at her feet was a flower, a whole field of flowers.

Trillium.

These were her flowers, her land—and she had found them—or perhaps they had found her.

Essie would love these. Stooping, she plucked the flower, one and then another, gathering the three-petaled flowers until she had a bundle of their white blossoms with pink centers. Walking back into the cave, she set them on the ground. Eliot had taken back his cloak and was watching her with curiosity, as she examined the blossoms and laid them out and began to weave.

"What is that?"

"Trillium."

"Ah, the flower of Chambria."

"Yes."

"And what are you doing with the trillium?"

"The first queen of Chambria wore these on her wedding day . . . which was also her coronation day . . . the day she became queen," she processed out loud.

"Trillium, on her wedding day?"

She smiled. "It's a strange flower, but . . ." She touched the three white petals. "She said it reminded her of the Triune God. The God of the Universe."

Eliot's voice was low. "Is He your God as well?"

She bit her lip. Two weeks ago she would have exclaimed of course He was, she went to chapel every day, she said her prayers . . . but ever since *that* day, she had not gone to chapel, she was angry with God, she had asked Him why—and He, the only Deity of Heaven and Earth—had not answered. *Will He ever answer?*

She continued with the story; it was easier than answering Eliot's question.

"She also felt it represented marriage, a three-strand cord not to be broken, the relationship between God, royalty, and the people, that they could not be separated."

Eliot's head had cocked to one side as he listened. "And you, what do you believe?"

She wanted to answer strongly—but she didn't know. And she didn't know him well enough. Would he rebuff her for her belief, or bolster up her weak-kneed faith? Regina glanced across the cave at him, hedging on her answer as she tried to read him. His blue eyes gave nothing away.

"I think, I want to believe Him, but right now—I don't understand why He allowed all of this to happen. What did my family ever do that we need to suffer like this? I don't understand."

His eyes narrowed and she wasn't sure how he was taking her answer. Eliot said nothing.

"What do you think about God?"

"Giving man free will was one of the worst choices God ever made."

"What?" She was incensed that he could speak of God so lightly.

"In my opinion," he added. "I wish I understood. I've seen a lot of the world, the people, the places—men make some terrible choices."

"And God? What is your opinion of Him?"

His eyes met hers. "I don't know if I have an opinion about God as of yet. But I do have an opinion of humanity. Men and women were created for worship, their soul must find something to worship. Some worship money, others status, belongings, family, their collection of treasured items . . . people will always find something to worship, the sun, the moon, the earth, the stars in their courses, or their king . . . but rarely ever God. Yet, in all my travels I have yet to meet someone who truly loves God and chooses to worship Him making the mistakes that the people who treasure money, position, and power make. They often have little, but they act like kings towards others. There are those who say they serve Him, but it's only lip service but those who truly worship and bend the knee that worship."

"And what do you worship?" she asked softly.

"I haven't decided. Once upon a time, it was God, then invaders swept in and slew my family—first time invaders have ever breached Falway—and the last." His eyes hardened at the memory. "You might say, I have been my own god since then, choosing to work for the king of Falway because of what it has done for me. The abilities I have—are gifts."

"And?"

"And what?"

"What is it like to be your own . . . god?" Saying it that way felt sacrilegious.

He shifted and looked at her, his eyes saying he was meditative. "I wouldn't recommend it. Serving yourself isn't as fulfilling as one might think."

"Are you going to change what you believe?"

"Bend the knee to the Triune God of the universe?"

"Yes," she whispered. Somehow feeling it was urgent. She wanted him to believe. That he too clung to the God she trusted—for she did trust Him. Deep in her burdened aching soul, there was a thread of her being that could not live without Him, that even the sorrow of suffering could not quench. She needed Him.

As Eliot had said, people were made to worship—and she needed something outside of herself to worship to cling to, to hope and pray to, and it wasn't until she stared her doubts straight in the face she realized her quivering belief was still breathing, that its grip had tightened on Him above all else despite the battle in her mind. As she had seemingly drifted farther away, He had somehow grown closer. Angry as she was at Him, she did not want to be without Him.

Impulse thrummed through her to slip out into the woods, drop to her knees, and to talk to God—to repent of what she had said, to ask Him closer, to lay her heart once again fully at His feet. To ask for His mercy—for the future, whatever it was, to be kind and swift.

But to slip out into the woods would mean to be followed—and have more than one set of eyes guarding her. There was no place to retreat to, this was the closest she was going to get to a prayer closet . . .

Oh Father, who seeth in secret, look into my heart and know all that I want to say to You. They say You know already but I want You to know and to be known by You—and You alone. Steady my heart to do Your will, and if You want me to be queen—place me on the throne, and if You don't—Father, may my end be swift—but oh Father please help me. Help me to know and to do Your will. Here I am, the handmaiden of the Lord, be it unto me—as Thou wilt. Amen.

The peace that glided over her shoulders and into her heart stayed as nothing had stayed.

She looked down at her hands. She had completed the flower crown. *Now, what am I going to do with it?*

She had prayed. It was obvious. Her eyes shut, her lips moving with words he could not hear. A change in her expression slipped over her features, there was a softness that he had not seen before, a peace. Grief was still there intertwined with pain—those were there even in her sleep, but the crease of worry was gone.

"What are you going to do with that?" asked Eliot, nodding to the flower crown that she was staring at in her hands.

"I don't know—it was something to do."

Eliot pushed himself to his feet and walked towards her.

"Give it to me."

She placed it in his hands.

Taking it for a moment, he examined the circlet.

"Kneel."

She moved from her sitting position to her knees.

He placed it on the crown of her head.

"I crown you, Regina, Queen of Chambria. Rise, Your Majesty," he said, offering her his hand.

A smile played at her lips, and she took his hand as he pulled her to her feet.

"There, now you are queen."

"If only my people would accept me as easily as you crowned me."

There was movement beyond the cave's edge. Eliot interposed himself between her and the entrance of the cave until he saw it was his men returning from their information gathering.

"Stay here, princess—Your Majesty."

"You crown me and then promptly forget that you did," she teased.

He turned and offered her a smile, and a single shrug of his shoulder. She leaned against the cave wall, and he stepped out to hear the report.

"Did you find Princess Esmeralda?"

"He's keeping her in the far west tower."

"Taking her out of town wouldn't be difficult."

"No, not if we used the back entrance and leave the same way."

"I need the six of you to take back Raven Castle. By the looks of it the back passage should still be open. Since they aren't expecting anyone to try to help the royals, the forest should be free of watchmen like it was earlier. Take it by noon tomorrow, raise the royal standard, and hold it for the rightful heir of Chambria. You four infiltrate the guardhouse by the tower where Princess Essie is kept and keep her safe. If anything goes wrong, take her out of the city and bring her back to Falway."

"You're going to go in alone?"

"Yes, I am."

"What are you going to do?" asked Victor.

"Tomorrow, we take back her throne."

ELEVEN

The banquet table was spread out before them, everyone was laughing and singing. Lord Powell stepped forward and held up his hand.

"A toast! I would make a toast to our king. Everyone raise your glass. To our king: his days have been long and faithful to us all. Now we salute you with gratitude on this day when you became king many years ago! Drink!"

She raised the cup that only had a sip left to her lips; it had been an unusual toast but one always drank a toast to the king. As she set her goblet down and a page came forward to fill it, she glanced at her father and mother. Her father's face was pale. The goblet dropped from his fingers.

"You . . ." was all he uttered before he slumped.

Mother screamed. A dart flew from a dark corner of the room, causing a crimson stream to bloom from her mother's throat.

Essie screamed beside her.

Men left their seats and stood on the tables, brandishing their swords, shouting. "Long live the Lord Chancellor! Defender of the realm!"

Chaos erupted. She clung to Essie, reaching for Richard—

I have to stop it this time, I have to stop it . . . I must . . . oh, help! God help me!

"Your Majesty, Your Majesty!"

Hearing the familiar voice, she turned to it. Eliot was standing there, sword brandished, his hand held out to her, beckoning her to run to him.

"Help me please, help me, help me," she cried as she ran to him.

His arm was around her, his blade held to defend her. "I will, I will, you're safe with me . . ."

His voice was soothing, the chaos dropped away, fading into the blackness of the night.

She opened her eyes with a start, a gasp escaping her lips.

"There now, Your Majesty," he whispered, stroking her hair.

She buried her face against his shoulder.

"It was a nightmare," she whispered.

"I know," he answered back. "You're safe now, you're safe here."

"I am scared."

"You don't need to be."

"But I am."

His arms tightened. "Your Majesty, I am here to protect you, and no one has ever taken a life that was left in Eliot's care away from him, by the grace of God."

Why does he make me feel so safe, so secure? He is so sure and confident of himself. I wish I had an ounce of what he has, then I wouldn't have to be afraid. They were seated awkwardly on the floor, he was facing towards the cave entrance, and she had her face buried against his shoulder. Regina curled her legs to the side so she could lean against him. She felt so small and weak, and he felt like a pillar of strength, and yet in his shadow she found strength. He moved and draped his cloak over her, hiding her from the world outside.

She was shielded, safe, protected. She wanted to feel this always . . . she wanted to be with Eliot always.

The thought startled her, and she pulled away.

"What is it, Your Majesty?"

She fumbled for words.

"You're still tired, you should lie down and get some rest."

Mutely she agreed and, lying down, turned away from him, her stomach twisting in knots.

How could I have fallen in love like this? How could I? It's only been three, no . . . two, I don't even know how many days—but it feels like months. How could I love someone like him—yet, how could I not? I do love him, but is it only selfish and childish? Oh God help me! I need to worry about a country, the fate of my little sister . . . and now all I want is to love and to be loved in return . . . by Eliot.

Regina lay awake staring at the stone wall, trying to sort through her feelings, resisting the urge to turn and reach for him. Sleep silenced the thoughts with a black dreamless blanket.

"Your Majesty, it's time." It was Eliot's voice calling her.

She sat up, and brushed her hair back, wishing it had stayed bound up in the braid she had done it in.

Eliot squatted on his heels beside her, a smile pulling at the right side of his mouth. "Sleep well?"

She nodded, not sure if she trusted herself or her words.

"Good, we are ready to set things in motion."

Six men had left last night, and now the last four stood waiting at the cave entrance.

He turned to his four men and nodded. They left and mounted their horses. Turning back to her, his blue eyes seemed almost grey in the stirring of the dawn. The smile disappeared. Her heart dropped in her chest. The time had come, there was no going back. When the sun set this evening, she would either be sitting on her throne, or lying in her grave.

"Regina, I have a plan to take back your throne, but I am going to need you to trust me completely with your life."

"Don't I already?" she asked, realizing she had given more than her trust to him; she had given him her heart. *Does he know?*

"This—takes things to a whole new level, and it won't be easy on you."

"I trust you." *With my life—all that is left of it at least.*

"You haven't even heard the plan."

She looked up at him. "I have none of my own, and I have nowhere else to turn."

The trust in her eyes hurt him. Everything he was going to do would feel like betrayal and if it didn't work . . . it would be.

"Do you want to know the plan?"

She looked at him, her summer-blue eyes trusting. She knew the cost of what they were about to do.

"Will it work?"

"Yes, it will."

"Then, I don't need to know. I would rather not know if it goes right or wrong, unless I have a part to play of course."

"Yes, you do," he whispered. "But it's not a part, it is who you are. The queen."

There was a moistness in her eyes at his words and she glanced away. He took the rope and held it out.

"Before we get in sight of the city I am going to tie your hands."

For a moment there was a glint of fear in her eyes, and then something else . . . something he wasn't sure if he could put a word to it . . . *it's not possible, is it?* He shoved the thought away. "You'll be going in blind, but I promise you, you will be seated on that throne by dark. From here on out, Your Majesty, you are my captive." Picking her up, Eliot slung her over his shoulder and walked out of the cave.

— CHAPTER —

TWELVE

His words took her breath away.

Either she had just surrendered her soul to the grave, or by a wild twist in her false captivity she would be made queen.

Her breath left her lungs again as he slung her over his shoulder and brought her to his horse. Securing her in front, he swung up behind and spurred his beast into motion.

They left the pass, and entered the woods, riding through the swamp and once again into the forest.

Here Eliot reined in his horse.

"Your wrists, Your Majesty." He tied her hands together with a speed that surprised her. "And now for going in blind," he said, slipping a large itchy grain sack over her head and shoulders.

As her sight dimmed, her other senses awakened and she felt rather than saw the edge of the forest and the looming city walls which seemed so much smaller than Falway's. There was the hubbub and commotion of market day that hushed as they came into view.

The silence that could be felt.

People knew . . . they knew who she was and why she was being brought to the castle. Her life was going to be traded for a pile of gold.

But the people supported her.

She could feel that in the darkness.

They wanted her as queen.

If the people want me—maybe I'll be all right?

They did not throw things, or jeer cruel words, nor did they cheer—but she could feel them holding their breath bated with fear.

"God keep you, poor child," she heard one woman utter as loud as she dared as they passed.

They had been incensed by the usurpation of the throne. It was only the nobles who had failed the people; the people were hers.

Eliot brought the horse to a sharp halt.

"Who goes there!" charged a voice above them.

They were at the castle gates; she felt its familiar shadow.

"I heard you were offering a reward for the princess."

Queen, you mean.

"Aye! That's right."

"Well then open the gate. I have her right here and I intend to get my reward."

Eliot's words tied knots in her stomach. *Have I been stupid and blind to trust him so willingly? Did I let love blind me all too soon? Oh God help me. What kind of plan is this? Why did I say I didn't want to know?*

They rode into the familiar courtyard.

Eliot jolted behind her, there was the sound of a thud, clatter, a groan, a metal blade being drawn.

"No one touches her, I bring her to the king directly to get my reward. Or I don't come at all," Eliot threatened, his arm tightening around her.

"Fine, have it your way," mumbled a man.

He had done this not a month earlier—to another maiden and delivered her directly into the dragon's den. No wonder Ransom had been so angry with him. Now, even his chest burned with what he was about to do. He fought the urge to turn his horse's head and spur it out of the city gates. Dismounting, he untied the queen from the saddle and slung her over his shoulder.

"Take me to the king."

The court was dining in the great hall. As they entered the new king was wiping his mouth and gave him a smile that made his veins boil. His hand moved to the dagger at his side, resting it there as if he was at ease.

I'll use it soon enough.

"I hear you have brought me something," he said with a slight wriggle in his chair like the infantile man Eliot saw him to be.

"Yes, I have—that is if it's true about the reward."

"It's true, very true." He motioned a servant forward to showcase the gold and jewels that were awaiting him.

Eliot glanced in acknowledgment.

"Now, I've shown you my goods. Show me proof that this is Princess Regina, because, if she's not . . ." There was the sound of swords being shifted from their scabbards as a threat.

Eliot smiled.

If they think they can scare me with that . . .

He dropped his queen to the ground and removed the hood covering her head with a flourish.

Showing a Regina whose eyes were filled with tears and terror.

His heart lurched.

Eliot moved for his tiny throwing dagger, in his sleeve, slipping the handle into his palm.

"Princess Regina, oh what a delight to see you. You've been running a bit much, haven't you. Now, Regina, I have two options for you. One, you can lose your pretty little head. Which I do think would be very unfortunate. Or what do you say to becoming my bride? Essie, I am sure, would love to see you. She's cried nearly day and night for you."

"How dare you! How dare you?"

"How dare I? You're in my throne room now, not yours. Your blood is no longer royal, now choose if you want to rot in a grave with your parents and brothers or be an ornament at my side for the rest of your life."

A solider burst in. "Your Majesty! They've raised the old royal standard at Raven Castle!"

"What? Impossible! Who would do such a thing!"

"I would," said Eliot, flicking out the dagger and sending it flying towards the throne. It found its mark and dispatched the newly crowned king instantly. The crown fell from his head to the ground with a loud thud. The court gasped in disbelief, too stunned to move for several moments. Eliot whisked out one of the daggers at his belt with his left hand and cut Regina's bonds, dragging her to her feet with his left while pulling out his two-handed sword with his right. He swung in a circle around them, sweeping food, plates, and goblets to the ground. "The same goes for any man who *dares* say that this is not *your* queen. What did he promise you? Lands? Wealth? Position? Can he give it to you now? He's dead!"

"Guards!" commanded a nobleman, and guards with their swords drawn rushed forward.

Eliot swung his sword. It was meant for one thing alone. They could not get near enough to harm him, and they were mown down like grass before the scythe. A second wave emerged and hesitated.

"Choose wisely! Bow before your queen and get your life, or defend that dead king and taste of his fate! Make your choice!" he commanded, drawing back his sword for a second swath.

First one soldier, then another dropped to their knees, placing their hands over their heart.

"Your Majesty! We beg your forgiveness and swear to you our loyalty!"

"Close the exits," commanded Eliot.

Instantly the guards blocked the doors and the nobles looked at him in horror. They were armed with only their eating knives.

"Ambassador," said Eliot, his eye falling on the only other Falway man in the room.

"Yes, Eliot, how can I be of service to you and Chambria's rightful queen?"

Eliot smiled. "Come to my side, I would have a private word with you."

"Of course."

Eliot turned to look at Regina. She was looking at him—he could not maintain her gaze. It was between awe, horror, and that other thing he had tried to ignore that morning. *You can't love me, you are queen . . . and I am nothing but a soldier.*

"Move the table and remove the impostor, bury him in a ditch," said Eliot to a cluster of guards at the far back door. They obeyed his command, removing the impostor king. Eliot then commanded that the chair that represented the throne in the grand dining hall be moved farther back and onto the raised dais. Coming to Regina's side, he offered her his hand, she took it, and he brought her to the ambassador.

"Queen Regina, the men of Falway offer you our services," said the ambassador. "If I may?"

She offered him her right hand, the one with her brother's seal on her ring finger. The ambassador raised it to his lips and holding her hand asked for the honor of leading her to the throne.

"I accept," she said and took his offered hand.

The ambassador took it carefully and led her to the raised dais and Queen Regina sat on her throne.

Eliot's eyes raked through the crowd, his eyes searching for the ones he knew by their expression were still loyal to her. What he wanted to know was in their eyes, rejoicing, relief, or hatred and smoldering revenge.

The ambassador returned to his side. "How can I assist, Eliot?"

"I don't know their names, but some of them need to meet their Maker."

"Cleaning house."

"It's what I do best."

"That's what I've heard."

"I want the conspirators first."

"Start with Lord Stavmyren."

"Lord Stavmyren."

"Yes," answered the haughty sneering lord.

Eliot withdrew a dagger, and sent it across the room.

There was a collective gasp as Lord Stavmyren slithered to the floor.

"A loyal one next," whispered Eliot under his breath.

"Then you want Lord Devroe, to set the example."

"Lord Devroe?"

"Yes?" quavered the young lord.

"Come here," beckoned Eliot.

With all the courage the young lord had, he stepped forward.

"Bow before your queen and swear your loyalty."

"Gladly," said the young noble, relief flooding his face. He turned with a smile to look up at his queen.

"Your Majesty, all my life long I will serve you and any and every wish of the crown."

"Thank you, Lord Devroe."

He nodded and got to his feet.

"Stand over there, against the wall."

Lord Devroe moved to stand where he was told.

And the ambassador gave Eliot the name of another conspirator.

The pattern was erratic, sometimes loyal after loyal would be drawn forward, causing relief among the remaining nobles to draw a sigh of reprieve, then another conspirator, man or woman, would meet their fate.

Eliot glanced through the remaining nobles; there were no faces that gave him discomfort.

"You've cleaned house, Eliot," whispered the ambassador.

"Very good, now it's time to set up her court once again. I suggest you be the rudder to the sails."

"While you are her wind," said the ambassador, turning and slowly going up to the raised dais.

"Your Majesty, would you like to assemble your court in the throne room?"

"Yes, I would."

The ambassador led the way, the queen leaning on his arm, Eliot a formidable barrier between her and the rest of her court.

"My sister?" she asked in a whisper as they walked to the throne room.

"She will be safely on her way to Falway by now. I will send for a messenger once this is complete. We must focus. My men keep their word."

Once assembled, Regina brought order to her court, replacing people in positions, setting up councils and councilors to help guide her and the country. She reinstated titles to those who had survived but been demoted, then set a date for her official coronation.

"There has been quite enough for one day. I'll see you all in the grand hall for dinner tomorrow. You are dismissed."

The court bowed and retreated, returning to their rooms to take in all that had happened.

The room was empty, even the ambassador left, but Regina had not moved from the throne. She sat sagging slowly against the back, seeming white and small, where a few minutes before had been regal and commanding, even if a little shaky here and there. But guided by the ambassador and the wisest of the council, she had done a great deal for her first day as queen.

"Eliot."

"Yes, Your Majesty?" he said, moving towards the throne.

THIRTEEN

E liot."

"Yes, Your Majesty," he said, moving towards her throne. He stopped at the bottom step and looked up at her. She missed him calling her princess.

There was so much going on in her heart and mind. She wanted her father, her mother, her brothers, and Essie—but none of them were there. But *he* was, and she wanted him near.

"Essie?" she asked.

"I have sent someone, we will have word by morning. They escaped the tower with little trouble. King Fredric will offer you an alliance with his son Wulf."

She nodded numbly.

So much death. She did not want to think about the blood of traitors that had pooled on the floor of the grand hall, once was too many—but now, she had seen it twice. First the coup that had taken her parents' lives, and now to claim back the throne.

Yet, he had spared her from sealing their death with her own hands and attending lengthy trials and dramatic execution after execution. The struggle for her throne was over, and it was hers. To rule and reign until her last breath.

Peace, through blood, had been restored.

She stared down at him. There was so much she wanted to say, yet she felt as if she had no strength to say it.

She needed strength, and she wanted to lean on his—but how to say it . . . how to form words.

"You're tired, Your Majesty," he said quietly.

"You must be too."

He smiled slightly.

She nodded.

"Do you need a hand?"

Biting her lower lip, she wasn't sure she could move, but she could answer.

"I feel weak all over. I don't know."

"It's evening, and you've hardly eaten in two, maybe three days. I think you're entitled to your exhaustion."

"Entitled as well as titled?" she tried to tease, not sure where she found the energy for an attempt at humor.

"Possibly." He smiled.

That smile, it unraveled part of her.

"Now come," he said, offering her his hand. Pulling herself up from the throne, she moved forward; putting one tedious step before the other, she walked down the stairs. Nearly at the end she stumbled. He stepped forward, catching her against himself.

"Are you all right, my queen?"

She let her head droop against him, her ear catching the beat of his heart. "Yes, I am." Slowly she withdrew, disentangling herself from him.

"I am afraid I must beg to lean on your arm."

"A queen should never have to beg."

She smiled up at him, looking into his blue-grey eyes.

"Thanks to you."

"It was my honor."

"I didn't know how much I could trust someone until today."

"You might have trusted me too much."

"I don't think so . . . Eli . . ."

Not even his name fully escaped her lips, before she fainted. He barely caught her before she hit the floor. The day had been long even for him—and she had noticed. No one else had ever noticed. Gathering her up in his arms, he called to the guards to open doors and send for the royal physician.

He set her down in the queen's chambers and set about restoring her as maids fluttered around obeying his commands.

Her eyes opened at last, and she looked at him through hazy eyes.

"What's the matter with me?"

"You're exhausted, that is all. You need food and rest. The maids and the physician will take care of you. But I am going to leave you now . . ."

"Don't leave me, Eliot," she said faintly as the physician ordered him out of the room.

The ambassador was waiting for him outside.

"I've heard of you, but I never thought I'd get to see your work. It was impressive but I am guessing what you need is a hot bath and some food in you more than compliments."

"That would be good," said Eliot, wavering for a moment—leaving her would be the first time he had directly disobeyed a royal order—not that he much cared, but this was the first time it pained him. *She is royalty and I am a solider. Besides, she isn't* my *queen . . . but I will obey. I will not leave Chambria until she tells me to.*

FOURTEEN

TWO MONTHS LATER

Regina folded the letter and put it in the bottom of the stack. Truly that letter was the least of the weighty concerns on her royal plate—but it took a great deal more thought than it needed to—she knew that much. She needed to make a decision soon. It was the third time that King Fredric had written requesting that she send Eliot back.

She had found excuses to not answer that question in her other letters but now she had kept Eliot in her kingdom and close to her side for two months . . .

Something needs to happen. But what?

She knew from her informants that the ambassador had also received letters requesting Eliot be returned, but the ambassador had not brought it up in any of their meetings.

Eliot was always at her beck and call, but—there were none of those moments like . . . when he had brought her into Falway and to her home. He rarely looked her in the eye if it could be helped . . . something was missing . . .

I need to let him go, but why can't I?

Her court and councils were urging her to send him away. They were afraid of him—and anytime he was in the room they were nervous. He had a way of getting information and keeping people in line, like she had never seen. He and the ambassador made a spectacular team keeping the court on their toes and out of trouble, and obedient to her as she formed her government. However, it also had the consequence of making her court childish and petty over trifling matters.

She brought him everywhere; just knowing that someone had her back no matter what was going to happen was an extraordinary comfort. The more she saw him during the day—the less her nightmares bothered her at night, not that anyone but she had put that correlation together. But more than anything else, her heart clung to him, and the thought of losing one more person she loved, hurt. But there were laws and edicts to be passed. Divisions in the court that must be resolved.

"Your Majesty," said her maid. "Aren't you going to get ready for bed? It's getting late."

As if to second the maid's words the clock struck eleven bells.

"A queen's work is never done; I've barely scratched the surface of these," sighed Regina, rubbing the back of her neck. *It's late and Eliot didn't return today. Why did the ambassador send him away on an errand? Someone else could have done it just as well.*

"But Your Majesty, you must mind the physician's orders. He said not to exhaust yourself. You need your sleep, and we need our queen."

Regina sighed and glanced at the stack of papers she had already reordered several times. She couldn't stall any longer, and Eliot wouldn't arrive at the castle this late at night.

"Is Essie sleeping?"

"Yes, Your Majesty, she went to bed two hours ago."

No getting out of it that way.

Essie had returned from Falway a happier child; Falway had given her a sense of security—like Eliot had her. *No, I can't think about Eliot again—but I can't stop, or can I? Can I send him back?*

Sleep was needed—but the nightmares. She curled her toes anxiously, hoping that they wouldn't be bad tonight. *Please, Lord, let me sleep tonight—keep Eliot safe, watch over him. Bring him back tomorrow.*

The doctor had given her something to help, but it had only worsened the nightmares. Every day she fought sleep as long as she could, but it came and conquered every night. Regina sighed. "Very well, I'll go to bed."

Like a good patient and queen she drank the soothing cup of hot chamomile tea, with milk and honey that was prescribed to make her sleep better and her dreams sweeter—not that it worked yet, but at least it didn't make things worse.

An hour later, drenched in sweat, Regina awoke, gasping.

Sleep is just not for me—not tonight. Not after . . . She shuddered. *I need out!* Slipping from her bed, she put on a pair of slippers and grabbed her wrap. She escaped her chambers without waking the maid.

I just need to walk and clear my head—and maybe my heart.

She went to her favorite window that overlooked the city, highlighted by the sickle waxing moon that hung low in the sky.

Regina stared at the rooftops of houses, houses where there were families, a family made of a husband, his wife, and their children. She wrestled with the realization that she was missing something, there was a hole in her life that only one thing could fill. There was a craving for something human that no one in her court could fill or even touch. Something like Essie's hugs . . . but even Essie's hugs, as sweet as they were, felt as if she was holding on to a black hole that wanted to swallow her whole.

She wanted someone who loved her, who knew her heart, mind, body, and soul. Who loved her for her, not for the crown, the wealth that was at her disposal. Someone who would be there when she woke from the nightmares, someone who loved simply—her.

Eliot.

A chill quaked through her.

He had killed for her.

Protected her.

Rescued her.

But could—

Would he—

Did he—love her . . . ?

She ran her fingers through her sleep mussed hair, stroking back the strands that had fallen from her lose braid. Leaning against the wall, she closed her eyes. In her mind's eye, he was there—he had been since he brought her home, since that moment in the cave when he had placed the flowers on her head.

Her court wanted her to send him away, and his king wanted him returned. For diplomatic reasons alone she should send him back to Falway. Her one security, her full and complete undoubted ally. *How can I part with him? I can never part with him . . . but how.*

"My queen, why are you awake?"

She jumped at the voice—her heart racing for more than one reason. "Eliot, you're back?"

"I came back late this evening."

"No one told me."

He looked down at her. "Did you need me?"

I always need you.

"I just . . ."

"Wanted to know I was back?"

"Yes."

He nodded slowly. "And the reason you're awake?"

"I—I can't sleep," she offered.

"You need to," he said, stepping close beside her, a flash of concern in his eyes that met hers fully. Her stomach flipped.

"What is keeping you awake?"

She paused for a long time. "When—when do they stop?" she asked, looking up at him.

He looked down at her and realization of what she was asking dawned in his eyes.

"Nightmares?"

Nodding, she closed her eyes and turned away, looking out the window before turning back to him, feeling the desperation for him burning in her eyes. "Every time I go to sleep, they are there. They won't stop. Why won't they stop? What am I going to do? I don't know how much longer I can do this, Eliot, and what is worse is every day I realize I can't do this on my own. I know queens have done it before me. I know God is with me. He is my strength—but I am still so weak. In my wildest dreams I never thought that *I*, little Regina, would be queen. There was Arthur, and then there was Richard . . . I was never supposed to be queen. I was never supposed to wear more than the crown of a princess. Eliot, tell me what to do."

"How could I tell my queen what to do?"

That little word *my*—how it made her heart ache.

"I just feel like it's shattering over me, and when I do sleep, it isn't long before I am awake again, they won't stop. I don't know how much longer I can take it. I see it in their eyes, they are concerned that I am going to crack and things are going to be bad all over again. They want me to get married and some of them are parading themselves and their sons, because they want to control me and the throne for their own gain. I am feeling threatened on every side, if I do this, then that noble will do that, and if that noble does this then this is how these nobles will react. They counsel me from one side and then the other, and I see the reasonableness of them both. I want to please them both, but also I can't. And I must choose what enemies I make. I think that is what hurts the most—I must choose my enemies . . . when once I thought they all cared. I must choose, and Eliot . . . it kills me. What if I make the wrong choice, what if . . . I don't want to make enemies? How can I rule when my court sometimes acts like selfish fearful children and I am barely not a child myself? Eighteen years, just old enough to take the crown on my own and not have a ruler over me. But I have not been trained or counseled in this way before. I was trained to be a princess, to manage a household and a household is so much smaller than a court, that and servants and items are much more apt to do as they are bid than courtiers. And, perhaps what is worst of all. They want me to send you back to Falway."

"What?"

"They think you and the ambassador influence me too much. That you are using me like a puppet. When you—you are the only person I know I can trust when I turn my back."

"Do you want me to leave, Your Majesty?"

"No, no, please don't leave me, Eliot."

"I have been by your side when you were weakest. I don't think you know how strong you are."

"Me? Strong?"

"Yes, you."

"I feel like a kitten who has no claws set in a den of dogs to fight my own fate out. One wrong mew and they might just have my head."

"What if I left?"

"Left?"

"Yes, left."

"Eliot, no . . ."

"You need to beat them at their own game once. Send me away. Make a public spectacle of me. Show them your strength."

"And what will I do when you are gone?"

"You will be queen."

"Who can I trust?"

"Do you think I would have left alive any man who would harm a hair on your head? They are afraid. They don't know you. They don't know what you can become. They are bickering to rule over you—when what you need is to show them that you are above them already. That *you* can rule."

"But why should I send you away?"

"Because I am a penniless man who lives by the sword, I have killed countless men, and I love—only one woman."

Her stomach squeezed in agony. "You're in love?"

The hint of jealousy in her voice pierced him. He had known, he had seen that her heart leaned towards him, that she wanted him by her side. But a love between them—the only thing that had truly kept him there was his promise to her that day that he would not leave until she sent him—and his own heart. He did not want to leave her.

He did love her—

But all he could offer her was his sword. There was no kingdom, no jewels, just his blade.

No, not even that.

He had already rendered her all that was needed in that way. And now that he admitted that he loved someone she was hanging on his words with all the jealousy of a woman in love.

A queen did not need a man's heart.

What have I done?

"Yes," he whispered.

"Who is it?" There was a tremble in her voice.

Do I dare . . . "You."

"Eliot, I—"

He cut off her words. "A penniless swordsman can never become prince, much less a king, and you know that. So, end this agony and send me away."

"But Eliot . . ."

"Yes, *my* queen."

"You may not be a prince or have lands and wealth—but you have a treasure that I cherish far more."

"And what is that, my queen?"

"Your heart."

She looked up into his eyes, twining his heartstrings closer to her own with her eyes alone. Resistance—he had resisted so long. Every day for the past two months he had wanted to confess, to reach out to tell her, to let his words out and now that he had . . . He reached for her, taking her in his arms, and kissed her—as he had been longing to kiss her. Her arms arched around his neck, and she yielded to him, rising on her tiptoes, returning the caress.

He pulled himself away. "Send me away, Your Majesty—for I have sinned. A good swordsman never kisses his queen."

"And the very best," she whispered.

"Sometimes forget who they are," he whispered huskily.

There was a long silence. Her arms still around his neck.

"Eliot, I cannot send you away."

"Why not?

"I love you. And this is very childish but need you. Only the days I see your face I sleep the soundest. If I send you away—I will never have peace again."

"Your Majesty, you can. I know you can. You're stronger than you think. I don't want to leave you, but Regina, you need to know how strong you are, what you're capable of. I am a crutch to you."

"No, you're not," she whispered. "You could never be a crutch to me."

"Then prove to me that I am not, and send me away."

Regina sank to the flats of her feet, thinking for several moments. "I will send you away under one condition."

"And what is that?" he said, tilting her chin up so he could look down into her summer-blue eyes.

"That you come back to me."

"Come back?"

"Give me one month to know my people, for us to understand one another. Then come back to me so they can see that I am not your puppet."

"One month?"

"Is it too long?"

"I am afraid it might be too short. I was thinking a year, maybe two."

"A year! Two? I can't live that long."

"How about ten months."

"Three."

"Eight, I'll not give a month more."

She pouted slightly. Weighing the wisdom of his words with her desires.

"Eight. It shall have to be long enough—because Eliot, I—I . . ."

"Shh . . ." he warned. "Save it. There will be time for that."

She shook her head. "Perhaps time for you, but there are words I wish I could have told the people I love . . . that I will never get to say to them. And I will not regret this."

"Even in eight months' time, when a handsome courtier has charmed you, and your heart from mine?"

"That won't happen."

"Won't it?"

"I am steadfast—you should know that about Chambrian women. We are steadfast and give all our heart to the one— the one we love. I love you, Eliot."

He stashed the look in her eyes, and the words from her lips in the deepest corners of his heart.

"When did you fall in love with me?"

"I don't know when, but I realized it, in the forest when I woke up in your arms, when you comforted my nightmares away. You are the only thing that has made me feel safe. That is a feeling that I am loath to let go of. At first I was afraid that my affection for you was childish like a toddler and their nanny."

He couldn't help his low chuckle.

"It's true, my move into being a queen has been so infantile. The more I looked into my heart the more I found you there. The more I realized that it was no longer a childish fearful affection, it was my heart that you possessed, it is love, a love I have never felt for anyone else in my life. I compared all of the men in my court to you."

"Do you think that is a very fair comparison to them?"

"I don't know. I don't think it is—because none of them come even close. Eliot, there is none like you and I want you to rule beside me, none other. Eliot, will you take eight months to consider what the crown has offered you? I will tell no one at court what we have spoken of, but you—would make me the happiest girl in the world if—if . . ." A warm blush was rising to her cheeks.

Surely the girl never thought she'd have to propose to the man she loves.

"Regina." He stopped her.

"Yes?"

"Always."

She looked up at him.

"Always I will be by your side, to protect, to love, to cherish *my* queen."

The blush brightened and her eyes sparkled.

"Will you be my wife, my queen, my everything?"

"Yes."

He dropped another kiss to her lips.

"Eight months," he reiterated.

"And not a moment longer. Then you must return, for we have wedding plans to make, of course. I'll have to propose to you again in front of the whole court."

"Is that so?"

"Yes, or they won't believe me—but you should act surprised if possible."

"Should I?"

"Yes." She looked up at him, hopeful, happy, a smile that reached her eyes. "Oh, Eliot, but when did you fall in love with me?"

"The night we fled Raven Castle, the fight in the forest, when I looked into your eyes . . . I just knew."

"At my very worst, you fell in love with me?"

"I did. Well, my queen, do you think you can rest?"

"I think I can now that you are back. Is this what it feels like to conspire in the dark?"

He laughed quietly. "I don't know."

She giggled. "I don't know either but if this is what it is like, I can see why people do it all the time. I rather like it."

"I don't think other conspiracies are quite as sweet as ours."

"I think you are right." She slipped her arm from around his neck, her feet fully settling on the floor. "Since tomorrow I must be very stern and send you away. I love you, Eliot. I love you ever so dearly."

heavy influence as you assume. Today I am dismissing Eliot from my service. He is returning to King Fredric of Falway with our grateful heart for ridding us of the impostor who planned the demise of my family and so many others."

A murmur of assent slipped around the room.

"So, Eliot, if you would be so kind as to step forward and receive this letter to take to your king for me, I would be grateful."

Eliot stepped forward to the throne and gave a low bow.

"It is my pleasure to do your will, Your Majesty."

Her summer-blue eyes looked into his, and his heart ached for her and wished for ten more minutes last night, one more whispered I love you, one more kiss to last them these eight long months. He took the letter from her hands and raised her fingers tenderly to his lips—it would have to last.

"It was a pleasure to serve you, Your Majesty," he said with a nod, retreated down the steps and out of the court, through several hallways and into the courtyard where his horse was already waiting—the ambassador stood waiting at his horse's head.

"So, she did it," sighed the ambassador.

"She did."

"It was a pleasure to work with you. Send my apologies to the king about never answering his letters about a *particular* matter; I shall do my best to amend it shortly, as the queen and I have had a chance to discuss it now."

A smile pulled at his lips. "I am sure the king will understand."

"I hope he does. If not, you might have to find sanctuary someplace."

"King Fredric will understand," said Eliot. "If not, it's not the first time since I've lived by my wits."

The ambassador laughed. "I am sure it's not. I look forward to seeing you again. Godspeed."

"Thank you, and to you." He swung up into the saddle and rode back to Falway, his heart staying in the land of Chambria.

In two days he stood before King Fredric, who glowered at him.

"First Ransom, and then you." He let out a sigh. "The least you could have done was written and said that you were wooing the queen of Chambria!"

Eliot tilted his head to the side.

"I am not going to get 'I am sorry, Your Majesty,' from you, am I."

"I believe the queen and the ambassador both sent their regrets. I don't believe you need mine."

"Of course you wouldn't. Now, you've got only eight months and your secret fiancée wants me to make sure you have some more courtly manners so you're not lopping off the heads and stabbing daggers into every courtier in her court, and that you can act the part of a prince. Does she know what she's given me to work with? Meanwhile I want more men trained by you before you leave. I know you won't have time to give them a complete training, but you'll have time to get them started, and the busier you are the less trouble you'll get into."

"Yes, Your Majesty."

"You start at once, so swipe that smug smile off of your face and get ready for work, you poshling spoiled brat."

"Keep in mind you're speaking to the future prince of Chambria."

"Until she crowns you, you are my subject; I'll speak to you how I please. You can write your grievance about how I treated you through the ambassador once you are a prince under his care; I am sure he'll be good enough to convey the matter to me thoroughly."

"I am sure he will be."

"Now go! You haven't been around to disrespect me for months now. Go, and at least try to be a good subject."

"Yes, Your Majesty."

EIGHT MONTHS LATER

Eight months to the moment he had left, Eliot stepped into the inner sanctum where the court was in session. A murmur of surprise rushed around the room as he was announced.

Eliot bowed low, dressed in black as he had appeared on the steps of Raven Castle months before, his sword strapped to his back.

"I was informed that you wished to see me, Your Majesty."

"I did, I do. There is a small matter my countrymen have been urging me to decide on since I came to this throne, and I have decided at last who it shall be."

The room was silent.

"Chambria, we are rich, we have everything we need within our boarders. Everything but a king."

"Your Majesty," burst in a councilor.

Queen Regina rose slowly from her throne. "I was promised this decision was mine to make, and I have considered carefully. This choice, I realize is not only for myself, but also for my country. If I choose a noble among my own people, I will slight one side or the other of my court, and since I wish to slight none, for that reason I have chosen Eliot to be my husband."

"So, by not slighting one side, you slight us all?" rebuffed a councilor.

"Perhaps I do, and perhaps I don't. You see, I am a queen—and as a queen I will have the joy and inconvenience of being a mother and bearing children. If I were to wed one side, they would certainly have the ability to push their side's agenda while I am indisposed with giving this country an heir. Meanwhile I know that Eliot will have no ties to be pulled on, he will rule in my stead with the firmness and equality that I am seeking, also I know that he will protect this country and the future it holds—Eliot is *my* choice, for not only myself but my country, for each of you."

"Your Majesty, don't you think you should consider?"

"I have been considering. I sent him away for eight months for this express purpose, to see if my heart held to him, to see if with him gone I could love someone else. But I couldn't. I don't. My countrymen, please, I ask you to accept the choice I have made—for all of us. I hope it is the choice that you would make for your own daughters and sisters.

Eliot I believe will have an impartial heart that will see both sides and help us find that happy balance as we move forward. Do you not agree?"

There was a soft approving murmur around the room.

"Your Majesty—we agree."

"Thank you, my countrymen, my brothers."

Eliot looked at Regina with a gleam in his eye. *His* queen. Queen of Chambria she might be, but queen of his heart first of all, forever, and always.

"Your Majesty, is it my honor and privilege to be at your service, and the service of your kingdom and people. I gladly accept your offer of marriage." And he dropped to one knee, pressing his fist over his heart. "I shall do all that is within my power to protect you and your kingdom and bring happiness to you, and your people, from this hour onward."

She smiled upon him and turned to her councilors.

"Rise, my betrothed, come take the throne beside me."

Eliot walked up the stairs of the dais and stopped to kiss his queen's hand before striding over to the seat at her left hand to take his throne.

EPILOGUE

Regina was reading over a letter from a concerned noble regarding his borders, when there was a soft knock at the door.

She recognized it as Essie's.

"Come in."

The door opened and Essie bounced in.

"What is going on?"

"Eliot said he would be waiting for us in the garden; can you come?"

Regina glanced at the letter. "This can wait until tomorrow. Let's go."

Essie squealed and took her hand, half leading, half dragging her to the private royal garden.

Eliot was there in the archway, leaning against the wall.

"My ladies," he said, pushing himself upright with a slight bow. "I am glad you could join me this evening."

"As are we," answered Regina.

"First order of business. Princess Esmerelda, I have a gift for you from Prince Wulf."

"A gift?" Her eyes lit up. "He thought of me."

Eliot smiled. "He has, he said I should give you this." And he placed a leather leash in her hands.

"Oh . . ." she whispered.

"Of course there is something to go with it. Casper." A full-grown white-and-gold wolfhound loped into sight.

"Casper!"

The dog lost all sense of dignity and wriggled in delight, licking the princess's hands and making small mad dashes into the garden and back to Essie, whining with joy. Essie ran into the garden with Casper.

"He's huge—is he safe?" asked Regina.

"I wouldn't have brought him if he wasn't. They are hunting and guard dogs. Casper will take good care of watching out for Essie; they had a special bond when she was in Falway and Wulf took great care with his training after she left. He has a fondness for dogs and is putting it to good use."

He offered her his arm, and Regina slipped her hand through, leaning lightly against him.

"I've missed you," she whispered.

"And I you." Eliot paused. "I found myself praying for you . . . every day and every night, and all of the times in between."

"Praying?" She looked up at him, a hope rising in her heart.

He turned, pulling her into a hug. "I've missed you, so much. You don't know how hard it was to leave you—to not be here every day, to trust you into hands that were not my own."

"Hands that were not your own?"

"Almighty hands."

She bit her lower lip. "Hmm, then, what is it that you worship, Eliot?" she asked, slipping her arms around his neck.

"No longer myself. I could worry all day and all night—but it did not make things better, but I could pray—surrender, and the more I surrender the more peace I found. I could not heal the wounds in your heart, nor hold you, but I knew that He could, and that He would."

"Thank you for praying, I know that they made a difference, and you were right—a month was a ridiculous idea."

"Hmm, did I come back too soon?"

"No, it is just right. Maybe we could have used more time, my country and I, but their wish for me to marry and being away from you any longer could not."

"And was there not a soul among them that stirred your heart?"

"Do you know that you're very hard to measure any other man against. They all rather fail in comparison to you."

"Should I be pleased?"

"Yes, you should be very pleased."

His eyes searched hers.

"When did the nightmares stop?" Eliot whispered.

"I still have them, just not nearly as often. Maybe once or twice a month. It was not too long after you left—for a little while Essie and I shared the same room—she is a terribly restless sleeper."

"I should warn Prince Wulf."

"You wouldn't—she would be mortified and—and . . ."

"You were the restless sleeper?"

"Perhaps I was," she answered with a bashful smile and a pink blush in her cheeks, meeting his teasing gaze.

"You were right—I needed time. I needed time to grieve, to know my people, for them to know me. I started going to chapel every day—and the words—*yea, though I walk through the valley of the shadow of death, I will fear no evil*—I walked that valley . . ." Tears came to her eyes and Eliot cupped her face in his hands, wiping away the tears as they fell. "He showed me that—He had protected me by bringing you, to guard and protect. Everyone gets to make choices—and I don't understand everything that happened. But I am grateful that I didn't have to walk through this alone. He carried me, and He brought me you."